Anthony T. Padovano

# A Path to Freedom

Anthony T. Padovano

Caritas Communications

Thiensville, Wisconsin

# A Path to Freedom

# Dedication

For Theresa, my wife,

whose whole life

is a path to freedom

for all who meet her.

*Caritas Communications*

*Thiensville, Wisconsin 53092*

*dgawlik@wi.rr.com*

*414.531.0503*



Printed in the United States of America.

Cover by Kelli Stohlmeyer, kelli@kel-i-design.com

Padovano, Anthony T.

A Path to Freedom

ISBN

ISBN 978-1-4507-7667-7

Dedication.....iii
Preface.....vii

**Section One**
**Becoming Catholic and American**

CHAPTER ONE
THE CONSCIENCE OF A CATHOLIC.....1

CHAPTER TWO
THE AMEIRCAN CATHOLIC CHURCH.....9

CHAPTER THREE
TO WHAT HAVE WE BEEN COMMMITED?.....29

**Section Two**
**Becoming Worldly and Religious**

CHAPTER FOUR
POWER AND SEX IN THE CATHOLIC CHURCH.....44

CHAPTER FIVE
THE PARLIAMENT OF WORLD RELIGIONS.....59

**Section Three**
**Becoming Faithful and Self-Defined**

CHAPTER SIX
HEARING THE VOICE OF THE FAITHFUL.....72

CHAPTER SEVEN
ENCOUNTERS WITH FREEDOM.....93

# Preface

Freedom is difficult to define, blissful to experience, arduous to preserve. It is no easy task. We must free the self to become something utterly unique but always in the context of relationships that attune us to the other. We can only be free in the restricted confines of our own lives and yet the culture we live in must nurture that freedom for it to have a future.

In these seven essays, I have sought to find a balance between the freedom each of us yearns to encounter and the freedom the whole human family aspires to experience. It is not one woman who must be free, but all women, for freedom to reach its fullest expression. Indeed, the more free one woman is, the more she is on fire to set all her sisters free. It is not one African-American's freedom which is the goal of inclusivity and equality but the freedom of all African-Americans which makes freedom ring and lets all know they are free at last.

We have been taught wisely that freedom liberates the oppressed and the oppressor in the same act of liberation. Freedom, ironically, is the most personal of experiences, and, simultaneously, the most public of our endeavors. It is lodged in the inner recesses of our hearts and in the public proclamation of our banners.

Being Catholic, from its origins, meant being free: from sin and death, from fear and insecurity, from being shackled with class and gender and ethnic chains. All these bonds were broken in a New Testament that claimed Christ was risen and invited slaves and Gentiles and women to the table of equality and love. It has been arduous for Catholicism to preserve such a vision and to make it work.

In these essays, I reflect on the demands freedom requires of us in our day.

The first three essays explore the theme of being Catholic and American. They deal with issues the early Church did not address as we see them now. Giving conscience priority becomes more urgent as Christianity develops.

It finds a unique expression in American culture which requires Catholics to preserve individualism and yet to connect with a global community. The commitments which result from this must be authentically ours and yet recognizable to a universal Church. An essay is devoted to the themes I have just expressed in the previous three sentences. The common thread is becoming Catholic and American.

The next two essays focus on becoming worldly and religious. Here too we deal with issues the early Church left undeveloped. It was not a community with strong authority structures, political influence, or elaborated sexual norms. Few experiences can entrap us more slavishly than power and sex. Power is oppression from the other which denies the virtue of individual freedoms; sex is the drive that entices the individual to have a lesser regard for others.

When power is oppressive and sex is dysfunctional, they leave in their wake the collateral damage of broken lives and lost liberties. Freedom becomes a casualty in the process.

Power traps the perpetrator and the victim in a cycle of violence and instability. So-called free love is neither free nor love but a flight into irresponsibility and exploitation. When power and sex are abused, and indeed in a community whose hallmark is love, they become allies of each other in an axis of evil. It seeks control of those whose sexuality it imprisons. When such a Church or community has political and financial influence, it may seek, globally, to control unduly the lives of those within and outside the Church.

I believe that a dialogue among the religions of the world and a convergence wherever that may be possible tames the dominating tendencies of religious communities by constantly offering alternative spiritualities. This dialogue also brings the wisdom of the entire human family into the definition of what it means to be a sexual person and how it is that we can achieve sexual responsibility by choice rather than coercion.

The common theme in the two essays of the second part is affirmation of the comprehensive human family and all the ways it seeks to be religious. There is something utterly catholic about such comprehensiveness and something inclusively Christian.

The final two essays are linked under the rubric of becoming faithful and self-defined. Once again, we see the antinomies and apparent contradictions of fidelity to something beyond the self together with a passion for defining the self.

The first of these essays is learning to hear the voice of the people at large who make up a religion or a Church. The best chance the truth has to survive is the community of people at large who manage to live life with a wisdom that has enabled the human enterprise to endure over the last 100,000 years. Whatever religion meant then is quite different from what religion means now. The common thread is the experience of the human heart and human intelligence which never irretrievably lose their way.

I begin this book with a reflection on the conscience of a Catholic. I end it on encounters with freedom, an essay on a very Catholic issue, Vatican II, and how it gave us a new path to freedom. The irony remains. No one could doubt that Vatican II, in every aspect of its identity, was Catholic. Yet no Council before it brought the world and the human family into its deliberations better than this one did. For this reason, it brought freedom into all aspects of Catholic life. It defined Catholicism as insufficient without the presence of other Christians, other believers, and other people of good will. Everything that was good in all these constituencies is already present in the human heart and in our common intellectual search for truth.

The more we behold the similarities in all of us the more free we become. Catholicism extends this to a similarity between God and us. It finds divinity in a human life and humanity in a God who made the world and made us free in it.

# A Path to Freedom

# SECTION ONE

## Becoming Catholic and American

# Chapter One
# The Conscience of a Catholic

The better educated we are, the more committed, the more difficult it is to remain institutionally Catholic. A critical reading of Scripture and ecumenical councils increases the dilemma. Many today know that unless Church doctrine is received critically, integrity and conscience are diminished. The list of troublesome issues is long and familiar: contraception and Christology, marital norms and intercommunion, mandatory celibacy and the refusal to ordain women, abortion in specialized circumstances and homosexual equity, a meaningful voice for the baptized and a collegial papacy.

Seeking to be authentically Catholic and honestly self-defined is a minefield. Responsible Catholics know that the larger Church Tradition must be maintained. The self must not be the only center; the contemporary moment must not be the only time-frame.

Good theology allows critical thought and human experience to coexist. It rescues people both from randomness and from conventionality. Individuals count, but so does the community. Doctrinal norms are unmistakably Catholic only when they are broadly inclusive.

The institutional Church, for its part, must refrain from the wholesale exclusion of people who wish to remain Catholic. The individual, in turn, must not be defined solely by what the leadership of the Church determines at a particular moment in its history.

I propose a five-part list of items that defines a contemporary Catholic. It is inclusive but clearly Catholic, distinct from Protestant and Orthodox priorities. Pastoral ministry today requires a validation of open-ended Catholicism and a rejection, simultaneously, of anything-goes ecclesiology. What might such a list look like?

## The Petrine Ministry
### As An Expression of Church Unity

The Petrine Ministry refers to how the Bishop of Rome, the successor of Peter, serves the church universal.

This ministry is open to a variety of interpretations, some of which are not Catholic. An example of this might be the rejection of that ministry as having any special or unique role to play, as in radically reformed Protestantism. Catholics maintain that the New Testament itself and, indeed, later Church Tradition, assign a role of significance to Peter and to the Bishop of Rome. The Reformation was a legitimate protest, at least in its beginnings, against a papacy that was less a ministry than an intrusion, less a sign of unity than a cause of division, less an office of pastoral care than a source of scandal. The Catholic Tradition does not accept the elimination of this ministry nor its reduction to a largely ceremonial role.

Another example of an unacceptable understanding would be a definition of the role that makes the papacy so central that all power and validation of what is legitimately Catholic come only from that ministry. Such an interpretation would assign bishops and church synods no authority in their own right. Pushed to an extreme, it gives a largely ceremonial role to the rest of the Church.

There is room in the category we propose for Catholics who define the papacy in terms of infallibility and universal jurisdiction. Papal infallibility, in its official definition, is far more restrictive than most Catholics realize, so restrictive that it has been used only once in the century and a half since its proclamation. Universal jurisdiction need not take away jurisdiction from other entities in the Church, even with regard to universal teaching. An instance of this was the series of national bishop conferences after *Humanae Vitae* which proposed alternatives on birth control not envisioned by that document and, indeed, differing substantially from it. Further examples would be the fuller development of the *sensus fidelium*, the consensus of baptized Catholics that comes from their lived experience. The convictions of bishops are also normative for Church teaching, so much so that it too is considered infallible by the papacy.

This terminology of infallibility and universal jurisdiction may not be the most appropriate in an age of collegiality and ecumenism. They need not, however, be eliminated totally in a large, Catholic understanding.

There is also room for those who define Petrine ministry in collegial terms. This more contemporary approach is also traditional. It does not favor the language from Vatican I and the century after it. It prefers the more ambiguous language of the New Testament and the more inclusive practice of the Catholic Tradition of the first millennium. Vatican II moved in these directions.

Vatican I, and the Council of Trent before it, stressed the centralizing role of the Petrine ministry. Vatican II, and the Council of Constance before it, emphasized the authority of the Church at large. All the Councils are part of Catholic Tradition. At some level of life and practice, they fit together.

The Petrine ministry is a touchstone by which the Church universal explores essential elements in the definition of what it means to be Catholic.

## An Expansive Sacramental System as Developed in The New Testament and Church Tradition

This is much broader than the traditional Protestant restriction of sacraments to two and limited celebration of Eucharist or communion. It is closely allied with Orthodox theology and practice but distinctively Catholic in its clarity of defining the sacraments and in their frequency. Catholics accept seven sacraments, celebrate them more regularly than other Church traditions, and give them a central, prominent role in Catholic life.

There is a sense throughout the Catholic Church at large that to be Catholic is to receive the sacraments. This stress on the validity and efficacy of sacraments is so strong that belonging to a community and supporting it are seen sometimes as less essential than receiving sacraments. The negative side of this is sacramentalism or even superstition, a disconnect between behavior and belief. The positive side of this is a Catholic realization that the sacraments are a powerful link with Christ and the Church. The excessive concern, at times, with who may celebrate and participate and how that celebration is valid or licit is due not only to a legalistic attitude but to an awareness that sacraments are events of enormous importance.

## The Core of the Church's Conciliar Tradition

This includes all 21 ecumenical councils.

This is quite removed from the weight Protestant Christians give ecumenical councils in general. It recognizes many more than the ecumenical councils of the first millennium that Orthodox Christians accept.

The core of the Conciliar Tradition does not include the complete work of each council. It does indicate, however, that these councils are matters of serious concern and that the gravity of them affects the way Catholics believe.

The range of councils is diverse; they correct and balance one another. The Council of Constance led to the removal of three Popes; Vatican I centralized the papacy; Vatican II defined the Church as the People of God.

We are not obliged, thereby, to accept the papal infallibility of Vatican I in the terms many people assume the Council intended. Vatican I was interrupted before it finished its work because of the Franco-Prussian War. Vatican I was completed by Vatican II. The core of the Conciliar Tradition is clearly not the total acceptance of a particular council. For further example, the Council of Constance insists that popes are obliged to obey an ecumenical council and indeed can be deposed by a council. Popes for centuries have refused to implement those decrees of the Council of Constance calling for automatic Councils on a regular chronology, without the need of papal convocation.

In another matter of controversy, the Council of Vienne (1311-1312) declared hylomorphism as Catholic doctrine. This teaching states that there is no human soul in a fetus until about the fifth month, that is "quickening" or until an adequate human form is present in the womb. This Council would not accept the idea of humanity present from the moment of conception.

A thoughtful Catholic believes in the Christology that emerges from the Four Gospels and, indeed, the Pauline letters. No responsible Catholic chooses to accept the teaching of only one Gospel or one Pauline letter.

This process of balance and completeness must be followed in interpreting the core of the Conciliar Tradition.

## The Gospel Mediated through The Life History of Roman Catholicism

Benedict, Francis of Assisi, Ignatius of Loyola, Theresa of Avila and Therese Lisieux; the social justice encyclicals of the nineteenth and twentieth centuries; Vatican II, all have a part to play.

The acceptance and later rejection of Crusades and Inquisitions, of torture and an index of forbidden books, of the sale of indulgences and the condemnations of Luther and Galileo have a part to play. So does the massive influence of centuries of teaching on Limbo, now declared non-existent, and of liturgical prayers for the conversion of Jews, now seen as an embarrassment.

The spirituality of nine First Fridays is vastly different from ecumenical spirituality. Prayers at Lourdes or at the Assisi gathering of all the world's religions, with the pope present, have a very different nuance.

An astute, balanced, responsible commentary on all of this needs to be integrated into the ways we accept the Gospel message. These events and more were teaching and learning moments for the Church. A partial or partisan reading of this history is not truly Catholic.

To understand this history we must not reject it too readily and, in any case, we must understand it, in the context of the time and the needs of a particular era.

Protestant and Orthodox readings of the Gospel are important and enlightening. But Roman Catholicism has its own legitimacy and contribution.

## The Spirit of Vatican II

Vatican II was essentially different from all previous ecumenical councils. Indeed, it changed, perhaps permanently, the very definition of what an ecumenical council is. It brought with it a "spirit" that went beyond the literal meaning of the documents. We do not speak of a spirit of the Council of Trent or of Vatican I the way we do of Vatican II. For this Council, such a term makes sense.

The elaboration of the spirit of Vatican II is an item of great significance for the definition of what it means to be Catholic.

## Conclusion

These five items form a contemporary creed that enables us to include a wide range of Catholics but not everyone. Such a creed allows people time to develop what it means for them to be Catholic, without the need to accept or reject uncritically the official teaching of the Church. Self-excommunication from the Church is far more prevalent than juridical excommunication. Jesus of Nazareth came to the table with all who wished to be there, with all who were hungry, not only for bread but for life.

A Church on the side of life is concerned about the integrity and the conscience as well as the compliance of its people. It becomes its better self when it refuses to rush to judgment or exclusion. It witnesses Christ to the world when it expansively invites to the table of sacramental communion all who yearn to be there, all who are hungry for bread and all who seek there a life of their own in the context of being Catholic.

# Chapter Two
# The American Catholic Church
# Assessing the Past, Discerning the Future

In 1775, there were armed clashes between American and English forces in Lexington, Concord, and Bunker Hill. The next year, 1776, as Americans know well, the insurrection became a rebellion and a revolution. One of the great documents of human history, the Declaration of Independence, called for a new nation. The Declaration was a revolution in its own right. It affirmed God but not the Churches, stressed the Enlightenment but not Tradition, and it underscored inclusivity as the operating principle of the new nation ("all . . . are created equal"). Never before or since was a nation formed with so much boldness and imagination.

In that fateful year, 1776, the Continental Congress sent a small delegation to Canada to elicit Canada's support in the revolution. For a number of days, Benjamin Franklin and two prominent Catholics traveled north together.

One of these Catholics was a layman, Charles Carroll of Carrollton, the richest person in the new nation. He had signed the Declaration of Independence, willing to face execution for treason if the revolution failed. He had also put his vast fortune at the service of the new nation. He had nothing to gain from this revolution. He supported it as an act of conscience. The founders of the new nation were impressed mightily by this Catholic commitment to what was then a very risky enterprise.

A second Catholic in the coach with Franklin was Charles Carroll's cousin, John Carroll, a priest, forty-one years of age. He was destined, as we shall see, to bring the principles of the American Revolution into the structures of the American Catholic Church.

Benjamin Franklin, a believer in God but not in denominationalism, a humanist who distrusted organized religion, and a very shrewd judge of human character, grew to respect John Carroll in their time together.

Catholics were not deemed dangerous by the founders of the nation. They were sent on this congressional mission of the highest urgency in the hope that Franklin's diplomatic skills and the Catholic sensitivities of the Carrolls might bring strongly Catholic Canada in on the American side.

Let us move our story eight years forward. In 1784, the American Revolution has proved victorious against incredible odds. The Constitution for the new government will be written and ratified five years later. It is very early in the life of the new republic.

Benjamin Franklin learns that the Pope is seeking to appoint a priest superior of the American Catholic Church. Since this is an age when government leaders were expected to nominate Church officials, Franklin writes the Pope and highly recommends that John Carroll be that person. The Pope agrees.

Benjamin Franklin, a humanist, was both a key influence in the founding of this nation and a catalyst in the organization of the American Catholic Church. John Carroll, unmistakably Catholic, was comfortable with Franklin, unmistakably Deist. They found common cause in the life, liberty and equality of the Declaration of Independence, which brought them together and helped to define them.

With this scene in mind, I would like to consider the American Catholic Church in the three significant phases of its development:

- The American Phase 1634–1850
- The Roman Phase 1850–1960
- The Catholic Phase 1960–Present

## The American Phase 1634-1850

After a voyage of four months, two ships, the Ark and the Dove, land in present-day Maryland. It is March 5, 1634, fourteen years after the 1620 founding of Plymouth Plantation, farther north. Catholics and Protestants crossed the ocean and together they created a colony where Catholics were free to worship. John Carroll will be born in that colony a century later in 1735. When Carroll becomes the first American bishop, in that same colony, in 1789, there will be 35,000 Catholics in a national population of four million (about 1%).

I have designated this time period the American Phase. In the first century and a half, Benjamin Franklin recommended John Carroll for a Church office and Protestants worked to create a colony where Catholics were welcome. Protestants were willing to do this about a century after the bitter excommunication of Martin Luther in 1520. In America, Protestants gave land for Catholics to build Churches and, later, sent their children to Catholic schools.

There could hardly have been a better choice than John Carroll to lead the American Catholic Church. His family heritage and culture were steeped in democracy and, as we shall see, in many of the characteristics we now identify as typically American.

Immediately after the American Revolution, in 1782, Carroll drafted a "Constitution for the Clergy" in Whitemarch, Maryland, after a series of three meetings over a two-year period.

The "Constitution" gives priests voting privileges in determining their ministry and their leaders. In 1783, Carroll writes that ". . . in the United States our religious system has undergone a revolution, if possible, more extraordinary than our political one." It is clear, then, that Carroll is deliberate and intentional in these innovations and that his model is the emerging American philosophy of government. In 1784, Carroll is named "Superior of the Catholic Clergy in America" at Franklin's suggestion, as we have noted. When Rome nominates him as the first American bishop a few years later, he demurs. He tells Rome that bishops appointed by a foreign government, albeit papal, will not have credibility in the new Republic. He asks that the clergy choose their own bishop. An election takes place on May 18, 1789, and Carroll is chosen 24-2.

In 1789, the United States Constitution is ratified, George Washington is inaugurated, John Carroll becomes the first United States bishop, and

Georgetown is established by Carroll as the first Catholic institution of higher learning.

Carroll allows English in the Liturgy and he supports a strong voice for the laity in the American trustee system. There are three characteristics of this trustee system:

- The laity nominates candidates as pastor and the bishop appoints
- The bishop has limited rights to dismiss a pastor
- Disputes are settled in an arbitration committee, half of whose members are lay

Carroll, furthermore, promotes open discussion and allows the dissent which accompanies it. He observes that "... a free circulation to fair argument is the most effectual method to bring ... Christians to ... unity ..." Notice the words: the best method is open discussion; this discussion does not promote division but unity. It sounds counter-intuitive to Europe; Americans know it works.

As we take our leave of Carroll, we note that a number of initiatives are in place:

- Substantial voice for the laity
- The right of clergy to choose their bishop
- A sense that democracy is good for the Church
- A written constitution for the clergy with a clear definition of authority and its limits
- A preference for public debate and dialogue on Church issues
- Ecumenism

- A warning that foreign and papal interference will diminish the credibility of Church leaders

## JOHN ENGLAND

In 1823, thirty-four years after Carroll's ordination as Bishop of Baltimore, John England of Charleston, South Carolina, issues a "Constitution of the Roman Catholic Church of South Carolina."

John England researched the document thoroughly, going back to the theology of conciliarism in the 1415 Council of Constance. That Council forced three popes to resign and declared ecumenical councils superior to papal authority.

This Church Constitution of South Carolina notes that the bishop is not the "deputy of the Pope" any more than the governor of an American State is a deputy of the President of the United States. As each American State can have its own laws, in general agreement with the Constitution of the United States, so each diocese can formulate its own laws and culture, in general agreement with the universal Church. The Constitution adds that "We are not required by our Faith to believe the Pope is infallible."

The Constitution calls for a vestry of laity to supervise the finances of each parish. The vestry settles salary for clergy and pays them directly. It selects all lay ministers and personnel for the parish; no lay person can be removed from office except by decision of the vestry. If the vestry has a problem with its priest, it meets without him and sends its report directly to the bishop for resolution.

On the diocesan level, a board of "General Trustees" is in charge of all diocesan funds. This board consists of five clergy (the bishop, a vicar and three clergy chosen by the clergy) and six laity, chosen by the laity.

The "Constitution" continues and advances characteristics of John Carroll's approach:

- A substantial voice for the laity and the right to elect trustees

- A written constitution
- A preference for public debate and dialogue

A special feature of this "Constitution" is an annual convention of clergy and laity. This convention takes place every year from 1823 until John England's death, nearly twenty years later, in 1842.

The annual meeting of the convention has a house of clergy and a house of laity. The lay house selects its members, elects its president and meets on its own. No act of the convention is valid unless a majority of clergy, a majority of laity, and the consent of the bishop are in harmony. If a majority of both houses disagree with the bishop, delegates can appeal to Rome to have the bishop do what they wish.

For some twenty years, John England is, perhaps, the most powerful voice in the American Catholic hierarchy. A sign of his influence is the two-hour address he is invited to deliver before the United States Congress. He will be a leader in assembling the plenary councils of bishops in Baltimore, as we shall see in a moment. These councils are the most successful example of collegiality in the universal Church of the nineteenth century. There remains an unmistakable American sensibility in the United States Catholic Church until late in that century:

- Nationwide meetings of the entire American episcopate, plenary sessions at Baltimore, convene in 1855, 1866, and 1884; they are consciously collegial in their approach as we have noted; they anticipate the national conferences of bishops called for in Vatican II.

- The American bishops arrive at Vatican I opposed to a definition of papal infallibility; they believe it will inflame American and Protestant fears of foreign interference, idolatry, and papal control of free speech; indeed, almost half of the American bishops (22) leave the Council as approval of infallibility becomes inevitable.

- The first Parliament of World Religions takes place in Chicago in 1893 at a time when Catholics and Protestants do not dialogue with one another easily; three episcopal leaders of the American Church participate, on an equal footing with major world religious leaders, much to the subsequent anger of Rome: James Cardinal Gibbons of Baltimore (from the North); John Keane of Richmond, Virginia, first rector of Catholic University (from the South); John Ireland of St. Paul, Minnesota (from the Midwest).

In these late-nineteenth-century developments we see a stress on collegiality, concern for free speech in the Church and a sensitivity to ecumenical and even interreligious dialogue. We find the roots of this in John Carroll's and John England's ecclesiology.

So what went wrong?

There are two possible explanations. The first is suggested by Alexis de Tocqueville, the most astute observer of American culture in history. In 1831, in the latter years of the American Phase, he notes that American Catholics are "the most democratic class in the United States . . . very sincere" but also "very submissive."

This submissiveness will end the American influence on the Catholic Church when Rome turns harshly against it. Submissiveness and Roman censure terminate the American Phase and bring us to the Roman Phase of the American Catholic Church.

## THE ROMAN PHASE 1850-1960

The Roman reaction against American inculturation is swift and harsh.

John Carroll is informed that he will not be consulted on the choice of future American bishops and that there will be no further clergy elections of their bishop. Some twenty years after John Carroll's brave experiment on election of bishops, four new dioceses are created and bishops appointed in Bardstown, Boston, New York, and Philadelphia, without consultation with Carroll or with clergy. The trustee system is ended and the ownership of all parish property is transferred to the bishop. Pope Leo XIII directs two negative encyclical letters against the American Church.

The first of these, *Longinqua Oceani* (1895) rejects the American separation of Church and State and makes it clear that this is a "very erroneous" arrangement even for the United States. The encyclical notes with horror that "State and Church ... in America" are "dissevered and divorced." Rome will at best tolerate this experiment in America but only until Catholics are a majority. At that point, American Catholics must press for a union of Church and State and for the marginalization of all Protestant Churches. The encyclical calls for a "submissive spirit" from the clergy and for "obedience from the laity." The second letter, *Testem Benevolentiae* (1899) took direct aim at American Catholic culture. It found American Catholics:

- Too eager to accommodate doctrine to modernity (change).
- Too willing to think and say whatever they wish and indeed to express these thoughts too readily in print (free speech).
- Too individualistic and too willing to rely on the direct influence of the Spirit in their spiritual lives rather than following the "well-known path" laid out by the Church (conscience).
- Too enamored of active and practical virtues, to the neglect of passive and contemplative values (pragmatism).
- Too dismissive of vows and formal religious life (individualism).

The encyclical condemns these characteristics as "Americanism," a general tendency to suppose that the "Church in America" can be "different from" the rest of the world. Cardinal James Gibbons objects to the encyclical in a sharp letter to the Pope on March 17, 1899.

If one looks carefully at the encyclical letter *Testem Benevolentiae*, the five criticisms of Leo XIII go to the heart of American culture. He dislikes, as we have noted: change, free speech, conscience, pragmatism, and individualism.

The submissiveness De Tocqueville observed and the Roman critique of America advanced even further because of the massive influx of immigrants. The immigrants were less adept with the American system. They did not, for the most part, have English as a native language; as Catholics, they cared less about an active voice in governing their Church than in surviving. A ready group of bishops moved in a sternly conservative direction, with Roman support.

The Roman Phase stresses submissiveness, the papal critique of America, and service to the immigrant community. In fairness, it must be noted that many conservative and even repressive bishops organized assistance for Catholic immigrants that was often healing and life-saving. A great deal of social justice work was expended on behalf of vulnerable and frightened immigrants. But these bishops, in turn, and many priests, insisted on absolute power and total obedience. They were brilliant organizers but also men of narrow theological vision. They tended to be belligerent, more impressive in conflict than in their capacity to reconcile.

John Hughes, Archbishop of New York, is typical. He dismantles the trustee system in St. Patrick's Cathedral, boasting, "I made war on the whole system." He added that "Catholics did their duty when they obeyed their bishop." Even more ominously, he warns: "I will suffer no man in my diocese that I cannot control."

Rome kept up the pressure. In *Vehementer Nos* (1906), Pius X writes: "...the one duty of the multitude is to allow themselves to be led and, like a docile flock, to follow their pastors...."

This Roman Phase was strongly hierarchical. It instilled a sacramental reverence for Church authority, a sense that Christ was present in every official decision. The laity were to receive authority the way they would receive sacraments. Obedience became a central, defining virtue, a mark of holiness, an indispensable condition for approval and promotion. Dissent was treasonous, diagnosed as a pathology. Initiative withered. This Church gave safety to its compliant members, but it filled them with a sense of paranoia and suspicion of everything that was not Catholic. It seemed a very long time ago indeed when democracy and open discussion were promoted in Catholic Church circles.

Nonetheless, immigrant Catholics found a harbor of safety in the ghettoes they built with their language, culture, and Catholicism. Within these enclaves, three objectives were of paramount importance:

- education and a private, Catholic school system
- submissive spirituality
- recruitment for formal ministry

## Education

The first of these was education and the construction of a massive and expensive private school system. There was a general fear of American culture and public life, a distrust of American universities, the New York Times, non-Catholic writers, and Protestant crusades such as the abolition of slavery, the women's suffragette movement, prohibition of alcohol, birth control, socialism. To many Protestants, Catholics seemed immoral, favoring slavery and alcohol and gambling, resisting a woman's right to vote and social reforms, using language against Margaret Sanger and birth control that was as incendiary as the language now used against legal abortion.

In fairness, it is important to observe that the Protestant majority did not always make things easy for Catholics. It could be discriminatory, even savage. In 1834, a Catholic convent was burned to the ground in Charleston, Massachusetts; in 1850, the Know Nothing Party was founded with a virulent anti-Catholic agenda.

Protestants were terrified of the papacy, now claiming infallibility for itself, and of the escalating number of obedient Catholic immigrants flooding the country. American bishops were trained in Rome and regularly traveled there for consultations with the Pope. Catholics fed these fears with huge parades like St. Patrick's Day and Holy Name extravaganzas.

There were Eucharistic Congresses in the United States which brought Vatican and foreign Church dignitaries in flamboyant dress and with aristocratic titles.

The Catholic school system never became as large as the hierarchy wanted. There never was a school for every parish. The American bishops meeting in the Baltimore Councils, threatened Catholic parents with the denial of sacraments if they did not send their children to Catholic schools. Nonetheless, most Catholic children went to public schools. Even so, the Catholic school system became the largest private educational enterprise in the history of the world. It trained five million elementary students at its height. This system was complemented with thousands of high schools and hundreds of colleges and universities.

The Catholic school system did a great deal of good, certainly, but it was under the strict control of the pastor, and this frightened non-Catholics. It pulled thousands of Catholic teachers out of the public school system where they would have had to contend with greater diversity. It paid its lay teachers one-third the salary of their public school counterparts and it gave multitudes of women religious virtually no pay at all. The system both inspired and exploited women; it gave lay teachers a noble calling but it allowed them no rights.

I stated a moment ago that there were three paramount objectives of this Roman Phase. The first of these was education; the second was the development of a piety that was sentimental, at times superstitious, and instinctively submissive. Once again, here also, not everything about this was bad.

## Submissive Spirituality

The life of Catholic immigrants was harsh, even cruel. People of enormous courage came to these shores, leaving their families and countries of origin often forever, struggling with language and culture, with menial jobs and unfair class and religious discrimination.

Sentimental piety brought comfort to many; quasi-superstitious practices, a relic or a scapular, gave a measure of control or protection; submissiveness seemed fitting (give us a church and a school, a network of friends, a sense God cares for us and we will obey in any way you wish).

This piety, nonetheless, fed, consciously or not, into the ecclesial politics of the hierarchy. It kept Catholics from organizing national lay congresses; it eliminated the last vestiges of the trustee system; it took away the will and the desire for democracy in the Church; and, it crushed dissent. It gave the hierarchy legions of docile voters who could be marshaled against political adversaries. It provided enormous economic clout to church officials who could boycott and censure films and books they did not favor. It garnered massive sums of money that bishops could use as they saw fit, with no meaningful accountability. The truth became a casualty through all of this. Cardinal John Henry Newman once observed that "piety and power make life difficult for truth."

## Recruitment for Formal Ministry

The third paramount objective was recruitment for formal ministry. At its height, in the 1960s, the American Catholic Church had some 300,000 women religious, priests, and seminarians. That number is currently some two-thirds less, with a much larger Catholic population and a much older corps of canonical ministers.

During the Roman Phase, the crowning achievement of the Catholic Church in this country was tied up with ministerial vows and ordination. Priests were called "other Christs" and nuns were described as angelic and saintly.

Marriage was considered an inferior vocation; lay life was a second-rate way to be a Christian. The juggernaut of a Catholic educational system, a submissive piety, and a denigration of marriage left Catholic laity with a diminished sense of their value and worth and with the conviction that the Church belonged to the bishops and pope.

Let me add, however, that the success of institutional Catholicism was stunning; no other national Church in the modern world equalled the power, wealth, and organization of the American Catholic Church. It also did an enormous amount of good. Its schools and hospitals, its rituals of healing and its parishes with their sense of belonging, its willingness to demand better working conditions and its insistence that Catholics must be American and must not press for the union of Church and State, all this was admirable. It gave people meaning at times and it strengthened the life of this nation. Such a Church gave us Dorothy Day and Thomas Merton although, we must add, it resisted the former and silenced the latter.

There were costs, however, and as Catholics became educated and autonomous, they were no longer willing to pay them. It was a remarkable system but it favored an aristocratic few and it eventually destroyed the freedom and dignity of people to an extent that assured its demise.

## THE CATHOLIC PHASE 1960–PRESENT

The American Catholic Church works best with revolutions. Two key revolutions define where the American Catholic Church is today.

We have seen how the American Revolution itself shaped Catholicism in this country. I suggest it would have given this nation and the world a brilliant model of creative theology for the modern era had it not been crushed.

The second revolution came in our time and we are its heirs and witnesses. This was, of course, Vatican II. It has shaped the American Catholic Church perhaps more profoundly than any other nation's Church. Indeed, it has both moved us forward and brought us back to our revolutionary roots.

Vatican II changed Rome itself and moved Rome closer to American Catholicism than anyone might have expected. Rome is now more defined by the American Declaration of Independence than it is by the papal Syllabus of Errors; it is more powerfully influenced by the Declaration on Religious Freedom, a Vatican II document Americans crafted, than it is by its own condemnation of Modernism; its present Code of Canon Law resonates with the language of the Bill of Rights and affirms equality, free speech, due process, freedom of association, freedom of inquiry, and the right of privacy (this is very different from Pius X's insistence that the laity must be "led . . . like a docile flock, to follow their pastor"). Rome realizes that the ideas and the language of American culture create a far more credible vocabulary for modern discourse than its own monarchical system.

Rome, I suggest, has no choice now except to move in an American direction. A revolution begins by rejecting the language of oppression and then compels the oppressor to change the system. The revolution has begun and it will carry the Catholic Church to reform and renewal.

Vatican II unmasked the liabilities of Vatican I. Vatican I gave the Church to the Pope; Vatican II made clear that the Pope cannot manage the Church.

The papal mishandling of the Church between Vatican I and Vatican II is breath-taking in its scope. The popes have been wrong on issues Vatican II reversed: political democracy and ecumenism, biblical studies and liturgy, religious liberty and world religions, Judaism and the Holocaust, the definition of marriage and the acceptance of married clerics, theological freedom and the overwhelming vote of the papal commission to approve birth control as a moral option in marriage (52-4). The architects of Vatican II were the theologians in the generation before it who were silenced by the popes for proposing the very doctrines which were now declared official teaching.

The last effort to maintain a Vatican I Church was the pontificate of John Paul II. He made his own theology and piety the norm for approval. Theologians were intimidated and excommunicated, books suppressed, male celibate priesthood proclaimed as ontologically superior to all the baptized, debate prohibited, women defined without their concurrence or consent, and servile bishops appointed in extraordinary numbers to tasks which exceeded their intelligence, their competence, and their pastoral skills. The sexual abuse by clergy was criticized in gentler terms than the condemnation of condoms to prevent AIDS or irresponsible pregnancies. Catholic political leaders were censured for their views on abortion but not for their support of the death penalty and their approval of war. The notion that the Pope is the Church and that the Church is a monarchy was revived under John Paul II but this time a Council, Vatican II, and a world-wide consensus resisted.

In June of 1995, twelve American bishops (with the support of forty other bishops who endorsed but did not sign the document) listed fifteen pastorally urgent issues which the American episcopal conference was frightened to discuss because of Vatican intimidation:

- Presenting the minority position of Vatican II as though it were the majority
- Ecumenical issues
- Marital annulments
- Appointment of bishops
- The relationship of episcopal conferences and Rome
- Collegiality in the Church
- The role of women and their ordination
- The shortage of priests
- The morale of priests
- The ordination of married men
- Sexual ethics
- Contraception
- Homosexuality
- Abortion
- Pedophilia

We must not, of course, overlook the good that the John Paul II papacy accomplished with its millennial plea for forgiveness for catastrophes and scandals caused by Catholics over the centuries. The social justice teaching which is a complement to the plea for forgiveness, remains impressive. There have been prayers with world religious leaders and support by the Vatican for separating Church and State, even in Italy. John Paul II and Benedict XVI, following his lead, prayed in mosques and synagogues and in Protestant Churches. There is the beginning of a Catholic bill of rights in the 1983 Code of Canon Law and a changed policy on married Latin-Rite Catholic priests if they are former Protestant pastors. Nonetheless, these changes have been made monarchically, not collegially. They are admirable decisions but they do not alter the underlying system and the abuse it generates.

John Paul II destroyed the effectiveness of the International Synod of Bishops, the most impressive collegial structure set up by Vatican II. The mandatum of episcopal approval for Catholic theologians, set in motion by John Paul II, threatened university theologians with dismissal and loss of livelihood if they were not compliant. The world at large does not see the Catholic Church as a champion of freedom or human rights. It is not friendly to women or eager for Christian unity. It has not been sensitive to the pastoral care people deserve if that care requires an inclusive priesthood or an acceptance of faithful homosexuals or remarried Catholics or a trust in the work of the Spirit as manifested in the *sensus fidelium*. At its best, it has been benignly patriarchical. In its worst moments, it has terrified God's People and tyrannized them in a shameful and deeply hurtful manner. The papacy is not a structure people readily turn to for healing; indeed it has left in its wake countless wounded Catholics, the collateral damage it inflicted as it imposed on the Church a harsh system of authority and control.

Since secularity and modernity have often been denounced by Church leaders, sometimes correctly, but often as a way of shifting blame and attention, it may be useful to reflect on the immediate past and to determine whether the world at large or Americans in particular are untrustworthy. The twentieth century was not only a century of unimaginable human suffering but also a century of revolution and freedom. We must not indict the crimes without citing the miracles. Nor must we be embarrassed if the miracles were frequently the work of American influence and democracy.

Three of these miracles are especially impressive:

- The creation of the United Nations, an American idea, in 1945; it has endured and emerged as the conscience of the world, sometimes witnessing against American arrogance; minorities and women found a voice at the United Nations never given them in the Catholic Church.

- The creation of the European Union, begun with the Marshall Plan in 1946, supported by Americans wholeheartedly and now autonomous of American dominance; the European Union has given diversity, reproductive rights and civil liberties a hearing they never received at the Vatican.

• The creation of democracy in Russia with the breathtaking collapse of Eastern European colonies (1989), the Berlin Wall, and the Soviet Union (1991), all in a two-year period and all without violence.

The fact that Americans cannot bring democracy or these miracles to the Catholic Church at large is the single greatest failure of American Catholicism. The fact that American bishops repeat enthusiastically that the Church must not be a democracy is anti-American and anti-Christian. All the other Christian Churches are collegial. Loyalty to Christ, after all, is not essentially connected with monarchy and ecclesial feudalism.

Democracy is not only the key to all ecclesial reform but the essential ingredient in global social justice.

No less a figure than Amartya Sen, the 1998 Nobel laureate in economics, insists on two observations of paramount importance.

In *Democracy as Freedom* (1989), he writes:

> "No famine has ever taken place in the history of the world in a functioning democracy."

Sen argues that the openness of a democracy, its accountability, and its freedom of the press make it impossible for governments to tolerate famines. Famines are the legacy of monarchical systems.

Indeed, we know that free markets are also crucial. It is antithetical to have free markets and not to have a democracy. Once the economic sphere is removed from government control, the government finds it difficult to maintain totalitarianism.

Sen argues, at a later date, that no multi-partied democracy has ever waged war on another democracy. If Sen is right and if democracy restricts famine and war, then a democratic world will be one in which social justice and peace may be possible on a scale greater than we have heretofore imagined. This is not a time for the Church to boast that it will never be a democracy.

American democracy has brought this nation enormous benefits. It may also change the world in a way that fits the Gospel better than any other governance structure we have known. This is an urgent hour for dialogue and democracy.

It is time for democracy to revolutionize the Church and restore it to its original New Testament charter of freedom, collegiality, and community. We need to decide now which tradition works better for our Church and serves its life: the imperial, feudal and monarchical system or the New Testament, modern, Post-Reformation, Enlightenment, American model of government.

We behold in the burgeoning of this new revolution on our shores the ghosts and memories of John Carroll and John England, of Courtney Murray and Dorothy Day. We see the inclusiveness of the first native-born American saint, Elizabeth Seton, who was Catholic and Protestant, wife, mother, widow, and celibate. We trace the journey to freedom as the Ark and the Dove drop anchor in 1634 and as Charles Carroll signs the Declaration of Independence. We note the Catholic connection with America at its imaginative best in Benjamin Franklin's nomination of John Carroll and in John Kennedy's inauguration as an American president who happens to be Catholic. We cannot forget the thousands of priests and women religious and laity who followed an African-American Baptist pastor, Martin Luther King, an American Gandhi, all the way up the mountain of freedom.

There is no turning back now, no way to stop all this. There will never again be a Roman Phase to the American Church. We have come too far, seen too much.

We are Catholic now in a way we have never before known. And we are American again as Alexis de Tocqueville saw us in 1831, the most democratic class in the new nation.

We have come this far with broken hearts and bruised spirits, betrayed too often by shepherds who became predators and preyed on our trust. But no more. We ourselves were not always sinless. But the crimes of democracy are always less than those of tyranny. We are free of that now.

We have a mission and a mandate, in independence and baptism, that will not allow slavery again in this nation, this time under the guise of religious tyranny. For we have been called to freedom by something even more awesome than our Declaration of Independence. We have been called to freedom by Christ.

# Chapter Three
# To What Have We Been Committed?

It was like a case of ecclesial whiplash.

Some forty years ago, Vatican II ended with a mandate to reform and renew the Church thoroughly, in all its structures and disciplines, making it inclusive, incarnational, contemporary.

Then John Paul II, for 26 years, ordered a reversal. Reform had gone too far, retrenchment was imperative, the Church must become conservative, even reactionary, selective, countercultural, exclusive, suspicious of the times in which we live. For a quarter of a century, many tried to run in opposite directions simultaneously. The ecclesial environment did not seem peaceful or creatively energizing but schizophrenic, paranoid, adversarial. It had all the fog and ambiguity of war about it. We had to work, with a liberal charter from Vatican II and a conservative, ideological Pope. We passed, it seemed, in a heartbeat, from Vatican II to a kind of Vietnam, from the elegant simplicity and clarity of a Council to a war zone with blurred borders, unreliable alliances, uncertain objectives. Enthusiasm and joy traded places with belligerence and anger. In fairness, some of this passage would have occurred under any Pope because the revolution was so rapid and profound. But it might have happened with a gentleness, a pastoral care, an even-handedness that John Paul simply did not have.

I would like to express how I think many of us worked through these dilemmas, made sense of them and learned to live with them. I shall consider three topics:

- Despair is in Order
- Hope is Justified
- What Happened and Who Are We Now?

## Despair is in Order

Although I concentrate on despair among Church reformers, it is worth noting that traditionalists also sense despair. All the Popes since the Council have been conservatives (Paul VI after his pronouncements on celibacy in 1967 and birth control in 1968; John Paul II; Benedict XVI). Four decades of conservative even reactionary leadership from Rome have left the Church in disarray and not returned it to pre-Vatican II Catholicism. Why is it that one Pope (John XXIII) and four years of a Council cannot be undone by forty years of conservative papacies? Traditionalists see despair everywhere. Stern policies, clearly stated, with the highest authority possible cannot win majority lay support. Papal policies with threats of excommunication and the intimidation of bishops who waver slightly on these matters have failed to unite the Church. A minority of the laity agree that abortion must be prohibited in every instance, that same-gender sex is always immoral, that contraception is intrinsically evil, that women must not and cannot be ordained, that optional celibacy will harm the priesthood, that divorce is never permissible. Blame is in order and so the laity are blamed or the times in which we live. But how can the Church get away from the laity or the times in which we live?

The traditionalist despair is widespread. Catholic publishing is permissive; Catholic universities favor dissent; theologians, priests, even bishops must be monitored constantly, carefully. Under conservative papacies, Catholic Church attendance in the United States has plummeted from 75% to 25%. The sex abuse scandal surfaced anger among Catholics so great that bishops are summoned to court, priests imprisoned, and dioceses driven into bankruptcy on lay initiative and with lay approval. Vocations to canonical-religious life have all but ended; such a calling is not even on the radar screen of young Catholics. Parishes close, seminaries disappear, Catholic schools end their service.

Indeed, there is despair among Church traditionalists.

But why are liberals locked in despair?

Partly because they gave their lives and hearts, their ministries and hopes to a Council that is now often regretted, even vilified by Church administrators. Forty years after this Council, there is no meaningful collegiality in the Church at any level. The laity who attend Church seem content with this, apathetic, unwilling to join resistance or reform movements. Only a shell and a bit of rhetoric remain of the collegiality that was at the very core of Vatican II.

The quality of pastoral charisms among priests and bishops has declined. One is now astonished to find a Church administrator eager for dialogue, open and fair. The claustrophobic ideology of John Paul II has been cloned and replicated.

There have been liturgical retrenchments, rejection of a pastoral sexual ethic, of an inclusive ordained ministry, of accountability for all Church administrators.

Ecumenical progress has been stalled for decades. Even with substantial doctrinal agreement among a number of Churches, Rome refuses to act. Inter-religious dialogue has been diminished by recent Church teaching.

Of the six great documents of Vatican II (Church, Liturgy, Revelation, Modern World, Ecumenism, Religious Freedom), only Revelation or biblical renewal continues to show life. The document on the Church has been shattered by papal monarchy; the Pastoral Constitution on the Modern World by flawed sexual norms and servile lay theology; Ecumenism by a denial of intercommunion; Religious Freedom by the denigration of conscience. Authority and canon law have become normative. This is not what Vatican II intended.

Reformers are aging and seem quaint rather than prophetic. Creative and pastoral dissent, once celebrated as Rahner, Schillebeeckx, Kung, Congar represented it, is now an invitation to the margins of the Church's life.

Despair is in order.

The few who remain optimistic appear desperate in their optimism, impractical, unrealistic, foolish, perhaps, arbitrary.

Despair is in order.

The Council is dead. The reform movement is finished. The renewal of the Church has failed.

## Hope is Justified

And, so, what does one do?

To join another Church is not an attractive alternative for many; to accept an unreformed Catholic Church seems a betrayal. This would make a lie of our lives and charisms.

Opposition to reformers is as hostile and mean-spirited as was that of some reformers forty years ago to those reluctant to change. A thoroughly conservative Church is as frightening and suffocating as a completely liberal Church.

Is hope now best achieved by abandoning the Church altogether for the sake of our integrity and authenticity?

Are we now called upon to be former Catholics or, if we wish to remain, submissive Catholics? Are there better choices? If so, they must not be fanciful or else we shall become foolishly hopeful and then despairing as the false promises and pointless visions vanish.

It is not the Council which undermines our hopes but the painful post-conciliar period. Let us, however, be more measured than this. Let us explore how this post-conciliar period itself can justify our hopes. We might do this by taking account of developments in this period, developments we take for granted, developments we found unthinkable even in the euphoria at the close of Vatican II.

- Latin-rite married convert Catholic pastors
- Ecumenical and Interfaith Weddings

- The Pope at the World Council of Churches or praying in a Lutheran Church to honor Martin Luther or entering with devotion a synagogue or mosque

- A formal apology by the Pope to the world for the evil done to it by Catholics

- A majority of Catholic laity in favor of abortion in some circumstances, homosexual committed relationships, a married priesthood, the ordination of women (even though all of these were condemned by three popes in succession)

- The legal status of homosexual marriages in traditionally Catholic countries

- A conviction, Church-wide, by most Catholics that one remains a Catholic in good standing and is entitled to communion in divorce and remarriage, in homosexual relationships, after excommunication, resigning from canonical priestly ministry without dispensation, after an abortion

- Catholics taking a bishop to court, favoring the bankruptcy of dioceses, forcing cardinals to resign in Austria and in the United States

- World-wide acceptance of the ministry of non-canonical married priests

- Organized communities of Catholics favoring issues Church administrators condemn while insisting they are Catholics in good standing

- A Pope meeting for hours, in a friendly environment, seeking no retraction, with Hans Kung, a theologian who seriously challenges the legitimacy of papal infallibility

- Assisi days of prayer with leaders of world religions gathered with the Pope as his equal

- A formal acceptance by the Pope of the Augsburg Confession, the charter of the Reformation

- Communion at the Vatican, by the Pope, to those who are not Catholic, such as United Kingdom Prime Minister Tony Blair

A number of the above items could have led to formal heresy charges against John Paul II or Benedict XVI by the Council of Trent. Pius X at the beginning of the twentieth century excommunicated Catholic theologians for less than this. In the United States, some bishops, before Vatican II, excommunicated laity for not sending their children to Catholic schools. That, at a time when excommunication was terrifying in the extreme.

Vatican II was not prepared to accept the Augsburg Confession or to have a Pope dine with the leading theologian questioning papal infallibility. It did not intend that laity would bring bishops to court or that lay people, opposed to Church teaching, would decide for themselves, without confession, whether they should receive communion.

A good deal of this is done unofficially but not without widespread lay and considerable clerical approval. The Catholic laity now see the world in many ways as Protestants or even secularists did in 1960. Indeed they take these choices as a matter of course, not worth mentioning. Large numbers of Catholics consider their non-canonical wedding fully Catholic if a married priest celebrates it for them. Such a statement could not have been parsed theologically in 1960.

I concluded the first part of this essay by citing six key documents from Vatican II. I would like to list now the five crucial areas where the Church at large is in a very different place from where it was as Vatican II closed. There are no structures to support these attitudes but they seem to flourish without them.

## Credibility

Catholics, in large majorities, no longer go to Church administrators for their values or their meaning or even their identity as Catholics.

## Collegiality

Catholics by and large do not agitate for collegial structures but they affirm what I would call collegiality by default. Their non-compliance serves as their consultative voice.

## Ministry

Hardly a Catholic in 1965 would feel competent to judge the value of a liturgical celebration or move from parish to parish until a better celebration was found or would attend a Protestant service and receive communion there. Hardly a Catholic would approve of a priest resigning his ministry or seek pastoral care from him. Catholics now, in escalating numbers, judge ministry by its charism and content, not its canonicity. There are still many Catholics who do not act this way but there were none who did in 1965.

## Sexual Morality

Sexual experience has become a right and not a permission or a prohibition. Catholics see this experience as morally evil when it is self-indulgent. The evaluation of sexual experience is personal, conscience-driven, perilous, but it is not for the hierarchy alone to decide or define. On every contentious sexual issue, the belief and behavior of Catholics is the same as that of the general population. This does not always make for enlightened sexuality but neither did the Catholic norms of 1960.

## Ecumenism

There is a general sense now in Catholicism that all the Churches are valid. The same is true of world religions. Catholicism is a choice, not because it is better but because Catholics choose to be there. Their children frequently feel comfortable joining other Christian Churches and an increasing number of Catholics find this acceptable.

Had we presented this scenario in 1965, most, if not all, Catholics would judge it aberrant.

All this leads to a deeper question. Are these developments tolerable or even praise-worthy, not because they emerge from Vatican II but because we have become secularists? Is secularity, not Catholicism, the driving force here?

Church administrators express concern repeatedly about secularity. They have a point. It is wrong or insufficient to define all human reality in terms of materialism or rationality alone, in terms of rights without responsibilities, or self-advantage without commitment to others. Such a definition leaves out the deep spiritual yearning in us, the pull of transcendence, the need to live with forgiveness, compassion, generosity, and sacrifice.

But secularity too easily becomes identified with its liabilities. Religion should not be judged this way. Nor should secularity. Secularity is conveniently blamed for the Church's policy failures and bad institutional decisions.

Secularity, however, is sometimes the honorable alternative to false and ignorant religiosity. It flourishes when religion fails, a symptom, of sorts, of religious pathology.

More than this, however, secularity is a value in its own right, a benefit to the human family and its religious enterprise. The Church resisted most of secularity's advantages. Some of the developments which came from secularity, with little or no help from the Churches were:

- Democracy
- Free speech and academic freedom
- Free press
- Separation of Church and State
- The abolition of slavery

- The rights of women

- Reproductive rights and responsible sexual autonomy

- The right of either partner to terminate destructive marriages

- The elimination of the death penalty

- The rights of conscience over inquisitions and the suppression of free inquiry

- A sense that the Christian Churches should not be divided nor the world religions in conflict with one another

- Workers' rights and benefits and collective bargaining

- Universal education and health care

- The legitimacy of the scientific method

- An independent judiciary

- The United Nations and the European Union

- Income tax graduated appropriately

- The rights of homosexuals to civil unions and the equal protection of marriage

Would we want to live in a world without these advantages? Often, church resistance to secularity tried to give us such a disadvantaged world.

Hope is justified, I believe, because the paradigm the world and the Church works with now, even when it does not acknowledge this, is open, resilient and inclusive. Closed secular societies (fascism, communism, terrorism, cults) are relatively short-lived and can only be maintained, however brief their tenure, with extreme violence. There is no future there. Science, communication, transportation, education, and economics require and demand global connections.

This same paradigm works also with the Church. No one claims Vatican II was a closed Council. Indeed it was so open that it concluded its work far more advanced in its decisions than even the most ardent liberal had anticipated. Despite occasional and severe reactionary moments, the contemporary Church works with Vatican II. Church discourse is conducted in the light of this model. No one quotes Trent or Vatican I much any more.

As we have seen, even a reactionary like John Paul II was compelled to conduct his papacy with far more openness than his instincts or ideology warranted.

An instructive model might be the United States Constitution. It emerged, together with the Bill of Rights, far more liberal than the American revolutionaries had envisioned. Yet that Constitution allowed slavery and excluded women from civic equality. These injustices were eliminated in the very name of the Constitution because the basic paradigm of the document was open, resilient, and inclusive.

In human history, paradigms prevail, and one can predict this, if they are endowed with certain characteristics. I argue that the paradigm the world works with now (open societies) and the paradigm the Church works with now (Vatican II) have these features. Indeed I would argue that Vatican II became the Council it was because it lived in a world shaped by the United States Constitution, the scientific method, and universal education. For a paradigm to prevail, the following characteristics are imperative:

- It must answer more questions and solve more problems than any alternative paradigm
- It must be clear and not require artificial explanations to make its case

- It must be theoretically and elegantly simple, close to life, so that people experience the paradigm as natural, logical, apt

- It must inspire creativity and generate it

We must judge, each of us, whether the modern world (open societies) or the Catholic Church (Vatican II) have any better or even viable paradigms than those we have just named.

Hope, I submit, is justified. Despair is myopic, unwarranted, uninformed, and unjustifiable.

## WHAT HAPPENED AND WHO ARE WE NOW?

Three powerful influences have shaped our lives and enabled us to become who we are: God, the Church, and our conscience.

We were convinced many years ago that God called us to the Church where we would find God with a unique intensity. Our love of God and the Church conspired with our life experience and conscience to convince us that this was where we belonged. This was our home. God, we believed, spoke to us through the Church and the Church was not at odds with our conscience. There is a powerful intersection in us of God, Church and conscience.

But Vatican II gave us a different God, a different Church, a different access to conscience and commitments and calling and promise. It gave us a whole new way of evaluating our life experience. We were not seeking this. It was the Church, ironically, which changed all this and summoned us in another direction, even though this may not have been its explicit intent.

The most startling development in this new paradigm was the Church's new understanding of itself. We had never anticipated this possibility. This new understanding jolted us, surprised and delighted us. If the Church saw itself in a new way, then the God it proclaimed and the human conscience it sought to enlighten would also be seen in a new way.

In a sense, the Church told us in Vatican II to see it as a less total reality than we once thought it was. Its document on the modern world, its instruction on ecumenism and world religions, its declaration on conscience and religious freedom taught us that the truth of God was in the secular order (even without the Church) and in other religious institutions (none of which were Catholic) and in our own consciences (even when the Church did not officially approve). Once we grasped this, we would never again be what we once were.

If our relationship with the Church is less total, it is not because we love it less or because we do not yet find meaning there. We see the Church as less total because we know more about its limitations, but not without gratitude for the graces it brings with it.

A child comes of age accepting its parents as less total, loving them nonetheless even as one becomes ever more conscious of their limitations.

Simply stated, we have become more confident about God and ourselves. Did Jesus of Nazareth not seek to teach us this?

Now we seek verification and validation not only from Church administrators but from the People of God, not only from official Church teaching, but from the Spirit within us.

We have found a new way of belonging to the Church and we were led to this by a Church Council. We did not seek to be there until Vatican II cleared a path for us, and urged us to walk it.

This is what happened to us in our post-Vatican II journey.

And so, who are we now?

We are Catholics who surrendered former patterns of living in order to reclaim gifts from our baptism and from our human experience.

Our ongoing commitment to Vatican II and to Church reform comes from our desire to serve God and the People of God without violating our conscience. It is energized by a hope of making our choice and lifestyle a prophetic testimony for the future.

We are also those who grieve over some aspects of our lost certitudes, safety, and comfort, the loss of the security from believing there was only one way and of experiencing the solidarity that went with it. We accept this in the hope that this suffering will serve the Reign of God and give concrete witness to our vision.

# SECTION TWO

## Becoming Worldly and Religious

# Chapter Four
# Power and Sex in the Catholic Church

## I. Power and Sex as Alternate Concerns

Sex becomes a problem when power becomes a problem.

The reason why the Gospels deal so little with sexual concerns derives from their preferred focus on power issues. Indeed, the New Testament at large has little over-all interest in sexual ethics.

Sex becomes a central theme as authority and power escalate in importance. If the power equation in life is balanced, the sexual equation is automatically adjusted.

Since Jesus resists power as a defining characteristic of his life, sex is not of utmost significance in his preaching.

Jesus rejects power for himself in the secular and religious categories of his day.

He does not want to be king when people offer this to him. He does not allow the sword even when this may rescue him. He tells Pilate he has no interest in political power but only in a kingdom of love. He keeps a distance from priesthood and wealth. When he heals, he does not seek submission from others but faith in God. The Easter apparitions are not a summons to retribution for his death or redress of injustice, but a call to peace and forgiveness.

The preaching of Jesus is consistent with his behavior.

If the Kingdom (Reign) of God is within us, then institutional or ecclesial power is less necessary.

If love is the hallmark of discipleship, then hierarchy is of marginal value.

If forgiveness is a sign of the Spirit, then the heart is where salvation happens.

If we are judged by God in terms of how we treat one another, then vulnerabilities trigger compassion rather than dominance or advantage.

One sees all this at work quite strikingly in Jesus' teaching on divorce.

It is not divorce as such that Jesus prohibits.

Matthew and Paul both understand this and write exceptions into the earlier absolute prohibition of divorce in Mark. The Catholic Church expanded these exceptions over the centuries of the first millennium.

The intent of Jesus becomes clear when one realizes that Jewish law and custom of the time defined a married woman as property. Divorce was an exclusively male prerogative of power over a woman who was juridically his possession. Adultery is not a sexual but a property, power issue.

The Catholic Church today sees divorce as an essentially sexual issue. A marriage is not truly permanent until it is consummated. A second marriage after divorce is allowed if there is no sexual relationship in the second marriage.

Jesus, on the other hand, prohibited the ability to own, control and dismiss another person.

Power over others, controlling others, is attacked in its very root by the preaching of Jesus.

Hear these themes in the light of later institutional, religious, and gender power over others.

- The Kingdom (Reign) of God is within you
- Love one another as I have loved you
- The Master has come to serve
- Forgive us our sins as we forgive others

- Come, blessed; for I was homeless and in prison . . .
- A man shall leave his father and mother and cleave to his wife, and the two shall become one
- Unless you become like little children, you will not enter the Kingdom (Reign) of God
- Wherever in the whole world this Gospel is preached, what she has done shall be told in memory of her
- Mary Magdalen announced to the disciples: I have seen the Lord
- Blessed are the merciful . . . blessed are the peacemakers
- Do not be afraid
- The Spirit anointed me to bring good news to the poor

## II. Sex as an Ecclesial Issue

### A Structural Reflection

Nonetheless, it is naïve, even perilous, to suppose that a movement with a world-wide mission could function without authority and law, structures, and penalties. It is necessary, however, to discern whether these elements have the same gravity as the Gospel which is being proclaimed.

Individualism, we know, is an asset of the highest order. It becomes, however, a liability of immeasurable proportions if it recognizes no responsibility for the common good.

If one could imagine the primitive Christian community, before hierarchy and monarchy, before clerical and lay categories, before creedal doctrines and canon laws, one might ask what its needs for structural survival were.

The community would require a structure to:

- Preserve its memory (rooted in Jesus and the apostles)
- Care for its people (through word and sacrament)
- Provide for its future (by development and new initiatives)

The earliest response to these needs is the Jerusalem Council in Acts 15, within the first generation of Christians after Jesus. These three requirements are addressed and a decision to become a radically Gentile community is formulated. Later, the first four ecumenical councils will craft the trinitarian and christological creeds. In the second millennium, three ecumenical councils were especially significant. The Council of Constance rescued the Church when the papacy failed and it established the superiority of Council to Pope. The Council of Trent responded to the Reformation. The Reformation called for a radical rethinking of how the memory, the pastoral care, and the future of the community should be considered. Vatican II was a deeper response to the Reformation and an effort to come to terms with the Enlightenment, modernity, and democracy.

History shows that the Council is the most sophisticated, inclusive, and influential way to shape the Church.

Power and authority issues are best solved in a Council. The papacy tends to use power absolutely and narrowly and it, therefore, gives us some of our most inept sexual teaching.

The Council is more diffuse and even temporary. It is less likely to seek absolute power and its very structure resists narrowness.

In an age of globalization and instant communication, in a time of democracy and universal education, the Council emerges even more credibly as the best structure for the collegial government of the Church. It must meet more regularly (every twenty-five years the Council of Constance decreed) and automatically (without a papal veto to delay it). When this power equation is addressed adequately, the sexual teaching of the Church, deliberated in Council, will be more healthy, less absolute and narrow.

Unless the power context of the present Church is reformulated, the sexual life of the Church will be dysfunctional.

Sex, we see, is an ecclesial issue.

The Council is the best guarantor we have that the memory of Jesus, the care for his disciples, and the future of this community are safe. The papacy is an interval office, even if permanent, to function between Councils, not a substitute for them.

## A Path to Freedom

The point of power or authority over others is their liberation, not their confinement; their autonomy, not their subservience.

Notice the behavior of Jesus in this regard.

He sends his disciples on a missionary journey where they are independent of him. He tells them at the Last Supper that the Spirit will not come unless he goes. The Spirit leads them to speak from their own hearts rather than in rote memory of his words. At the end, bread and wine, discipleship and sacrament, not structures, directives and rules, become the means by which memory is preserved, care is given, and the future assured. Jesus does not lecture but speaks of faith in God and of his faith in the disciples.

It is true, of course, that structures and imperatives are not alien to discipleship and sacrament, but the stress ought to be on the capacity of the community and the individual to find their way without excessive interference from those in power. This includes the discovery of one's own sexual path. The integrity of a relationship assures sexual fidelity far more effectively than institutional structures.

The Church, seen as institution and structure, is made marginal by the behavior and teaching of Jesus. In much the same manner, a mother becomes marginal to a child's life once adulthood is achieved.

Democracy is a political way of allowing the State to become marginal to a citizen whose freedom and rights, whose choices and values are paramount. Christianity does its work best by making the Church marginal to a believer whose conscience and calling, whose belief and ethics, personally formulated, matter more. It is not conformity but remaining in the large context of the Church's tradition which makes a Catholic truly Catholic.

Stress on the self does not necessarily lead to self-centeredness. Children do not become egocentric by disengaging from their parents. Democracies do not engender self-indulgence. Nor do they create conditions which destabilize community structures. Indeed, monarchies are more prone to indulgence and instability.

The Church drifted into monarchical and hierarchical structures not because these structures have a biblical mandate, but because they reflected the Roman imperial culture of the time. The Church is far more decisively shaped by history than its administrators sometimes realize. These aristocratic structures may even have served pastoral purposes in their time and on occasion. They are not, however, essential to the Church and, indeed, in the modern world may well impede its mission.

The parables and metaphors of the Gospel marginalize the Church and address the heart of the hearer.

It is not obedience to the father but forgiveness of the wayward son which reflects more deeply God's will for the Church. The spontaneous human desire to rescue, in the parable of the Good Samaritan, sets a pattern for the Church.

One must light the lamp of one's own life, open the door of one's own heart, decide whether one has the resources to build, and search out, on one's own initiative, the lost sheep, even if it endangers for a time those sheep which are safe and comfortable. It is not submissiveness but personal calling which leads us to invest our talents wisely, to love those who harm us and to follow a prophet whom the religious institution of the day rejects.

Sexual issues, likewise, are dealt with best in a community which does not dominate and control. The question is not whether sexual activity becomes readily too self-indulgent in the present but whether it was sufficiently personalized in earlier centuries.

If, for example, sex is a man's prerogative and a woman's obligation, if sex favors the creation of male children, then sex is already depersonalized even, of course, before Christianity comes on the scene. Christianity often reinforced male privileges and, furthermore, defined propagation as the essential value which legitimized sex. Abortion, contraception, homosexuality, and masturbation will be rejected because they do not lead to propagation.

Christianity adds to the burden of sexuality a number of especially dysfunctional impediments. It teaches over the centuries:

- The evil of pleasure in sexuality and the need to reduce this pleasure or eliminate it altogether

- The transmission of original sin through the sexual acts which lead to conception (St. Augustine)

- The ideal of an utterly sexless life (Council of Trent)

- The validation of all these teachings as God's will

For many Christians, over the centuries, it was not their lack of faith and love which seemed to determine their salvation but their sexual behavior. Indeed, this behavior never admitted what was called "poverty of material." The slightest sexual pleasure, even a thought too long permitted, was grave matter, mortal sin, and merited eternal damnation. If the Church is seen as necessary for salvation, and if this Church makes sexuality a central theme of its teaching, then sexuality is profoundly depersonalized and, indeed, becomes not a gift from God but something perilous in the extreme.

The sexual revolution of the twentieth century was possible because the Churches lost their legitimacy in defining sexual behavior and mediating spirituality exclusively. Although no responsible person endorses the excesses of this sexual revolution, no responsible person, I suggest, wants to return to the sexual repression and negativity of previous centuries. Nor indeed to the dominance the institutional Church once had. Women could not be liberated until sex was liberated from ecclesial confinement and until the Church itself was liberated from its own pretensions to divinity. This is one reason why the sexual revolution and women's liberation happened outside the Church. The first casualty, even if not the intended target, of these freedom movements was a Church which saw itself as central in everyone's lives and as indispensable to God's plan.

Revolutions, nonetheless, never bring us utopia. The marginalization of the Church and the personalization of sexual choices have their own liabilities. We shall see later how the Church itself still has an important role to play in our lives and how sexuality must still be subjected to some community standards. For the moment, it is necessary to stress that the marginalization of the Church and the sexual liberation of the present age are not necessarily evils or signs of decadence or even secularity but may be signs of grace, development, and virtue.

It is not only improper sexual expression but, even more tellingly, enforced repression which creates sexual abuse. A system which claims that all pregnancies must come to term, that all acts of marital intercourse must be open to conception, that masturbation is always intrinsically disordered, and homosexual activity essentially perverted, a system which claims all this and allows no exceptions or qualification, no nuance or resiliency, a system which insists, furthermore, that this is God's will for everyone and that it knows this infallibly and that salvation itself is at issue in these directives, such a system, I believe, does incalculably more damage to people than sexual permissiveness does. Neither rigid sexual control nor license is the ideal but one, I submit, is far worse than the other.

Correlatively, the repeated teaching that only one religion is salvific and that only one Church is true is an invitation to arrogance at best and violence on occasion. If unrealistic and depersonalized sexual norms oppress the individual, "true" Churches oppress the human family. Depersonalized sexual norms make individuals the victims of biology or of Church policies. "True" Churches oppose the spirituality of which the human family is capable, a spirituality which enriches everyone when it is honored and harms everyone when it is dismissed.

Sex, is, indeed, an ecclesial issue. It is, however, as we shall see now, even more than this.

## III. Sex is a Christological Issue

If the point of Christology is a revelation of our fundamental anthropology, then here too we gain insight into our sexuality. The Christological question is, therefore, not marginal for either Christians or, indeed, for the whole human family.

What are some of the insights that the incarnation of God in human life offers us? We might say immediately that incarnation means that human life is essentially divine and sacramental. If in the depths of our being, grace and the presence of God are possible, then our humanity exceeds our capacity to quantify and secularize it. In this sense, human rights are not only politically grounded, they flow from our very humanity. These rights are not a privilege but an imperative. There is no healthy human life without them.

If God is present in human life, then God is worshipped as human life is served and as its essential integrity is preserved.

Christology tells us that the human heart is more sacred than our Scriptures or sacraments or Churches. God creates the human heart. Biblical, ritual, religious, institutional developments come later. The whole human family knows the human heart. The later developments are less known and frequently divisive.

There is no adequate way of defining human life except through sexual categories. Sexuality forces our definitions to become concrete and rescues them from abstractions. It gives God the human face Christology requires.

Without sexuality, there is literally no future for the human family. Without sexuality, our sense of love is less intense. Without sexuality, our definition of God is less intimate. Without sexuality, God cannot be defined as lover, spouse, mother, father but only as friend, companion or, more remotely, overseer and judge. God as creator is conceived of very differently if we ourselves have no capacity to conceive life.

Human rights, then, demand reproductive rights. These reproductive rights honor us as creators and, indeed, as saviors. Salvation means to rescue and preserve. The most enduring and universally comprehensible image of salvation is the parent rescuing and preserving the child the parent sexually generated. The giving of one's own life for one's children is understandable in every part of the world. Such a parent is honored everywhere.

A God who might do the same for us is a God we can hardly keep from loving. The divinity and sacramental dimensions of human life are Christology's first revelation to us.

There is more, however.

Christology tells us that the motive behind incarnation is love, not truth or the elimination of error or the removal of sin, but love. All other consequences of incarnation must follow love. Otherwise we have a God who is a philosopher or a supervisor but not a lover. And, then, we have no authentic Christology.

If God is a lover of us, then, God has always been human. Love, therefore, is as much a human event as it is a divine initiative.

If the point of the incarnation is love and if love is essential to our humanity, then love is the essence of our sexuality. It is not incidental that sex is called "making love" and that sexual fidelity grounds all our relationships. Sex is preeminently the sacrament of life. All know this. It is also love's privileged expression. In the modern world, we have come to understand this better than we did in the past. This understanding drives the reform of our Churches and of our gender definitions. It has led us to redefine marriage and ourselves and morality and God.

Sex abuse, then, is a crime against humanity, a Christological violation, an ecclesial assault, a profound rejection of the humanity of others and of the divinity within them. When our sexuality is handled badly, it is, therefore, not sex which is disordered but our very humanity. Sex is dealt with dysfunctionally not only in overt abuse but in covert repression. A repressed sexuality is a repressed humanity. It leads to abuse and anger, to power games and rape, to a lust for dominating and controlling, to self-righteousness and hypocrisy. At the heart of all ecclesial corruption is sexual corruption. At the core of all Christological heresy is the violation of the human heart. At the center of all human crime and sin and evil is the denial of our human and reproductive rights.

Sex is kept in check, so to speak, given the boundaries all human deeds require, not by norms extrinsic to it but by its own essence, which is love. Love is the only issue which truly interests us; it is the experience which most fascinates and attracts us; it is that before which we are perennially vulnerable and always moved. Sex intrigues us so much because we were made for love. The point of falling in love is making love. The point of making love is keeping us from falling out of love.

Celibacy is useless as sexual control. It is only helpful when it, too, becomes an act of love and approximates as closely as possible sexual love. Celibacy, therefore, must be free and therefore provisional, intimate and tactile (even if not genital), committed to community and rooted in that fidelity by which we give ourselves to others. Celibacy cannot be juridically imposed in a healthy manner. Like sex and marriage, it is existentially vitalizing or it is vitiated in its very essence. Celibacy is the prolongation of the sexual intervals one finds in all marriages for as long as this is required for the freedom and integrity of the celibate. Celibacy, by any other means, is sexual abuse.

We may choose not to exercise our human and sexual and reproductive rights but they cannot be justly taken from us.

A Church which makes a business of sexual repression and mandatory celibacy creates disorder in its structures and dysfunctionality in the Christology it proclaims. It is impossible to have a community without pleasure. The pleasure of eating makes eating a social bond. The pleasure of sex makes sex an act of love. Indeed, the pleasure of not having sex when this is inappropriate makes celibacy and friendship a graced possibility. There is no community without pleasure. Therefore, there is no marriage, except in the most bizarre juridical definition of it, when the pleasure of eating together and sleeping together are gone. It is naïve, of course, to suppose that there is never distress and distance in a marital relationship. The over-all environment of marriage, however, must give pleasure if that marriage is truly what it claims to be.

The body is radically relational (we see this most clearly in sex and in pregnancy) and it is, therefore, radically sexual.

It is not pleasure which is dangerous but the refusal to connect.

If Christ gives us a model of poverty, chastity and obedience, it is not because possessions and sexual pleasure and autonomy are vices. It is because love, of its very nature, turns concomitantly to frugality and generosity. Poverty increases the joy of possessions; restraint makes sexual pleasure more intense; listening to another allows one's own voice to find its authentic expression.

In just such a manner is community engendered, not by rules but by the sheer force of its own love.

The fundamental value of all Christology is human community. When that community is genuine, humanity discovers its divinity and the demons of power and sexual dysfunctionality are expelled. Unless there is a viable human community, our Christology has nowhere to go and incarnation becomes an impossibility.

## IV. Experience and Revelation

Experience is the way we become human. It is constantly revelatory, from consciousness to knowledge, through reason and moral awareness, into mysticism and memory.

The most convincing testimony of the truth, today, is not authority or logic, Scripture or tradition.

Experience is more persuasive than anything else.

Let us look briefly at what experience reveals to us of responsible sexuality and the role of religion.

First, responsible sexuality.

The Global Ethic, promulgated by the Parliament of World Religions, makes clear that all religious systems call for responsible sexuality. No culture has given total endorsement to all sexual activity or allowed individuals to determine, purely on their own authority, what we may do with our sexuality. There are sexual norms and prohibitions even without religion.

Sexual guidelines originate from our experience, long before they are institutionally formulated.

Contemporary experience stresses, as never before, that reproductive rights belong to the individual and that their responsible expression requires mutuality and community standards. There have always been community standards, as we have seen. The new awareness in our experience of sexuality is a stress on rights and on mutuality. If community standards seem less stringent today, rights and mutuality are emphasized as never before in history. Rights pertain to the individual; mutuality, to the other person. Reproductive rights declare that the individual makes the decision for sexual experience and determines the timing and number of children. These rights do not require, as in the past, that pleasure and bonding be subordinated to propagation.

An analogy might be made here with free speech. People have a right to speak freely. This right cannot be justly abrogated. It must, however, regard the mutuality of the other's right to free speech and it must fit in with community norms. For example, one has no right to defame or degrade the other. Free speech intends self-expression and integrity, not an assault on others.

Reproductive rights are a new category in human thought. Reproduction was once seen preeminently as a duty or community dictate. Today people are aware that the survival of the human family is not at issue in our sexuality the way it was. Indeed it is not reproduction but responsible sexuality which defines people more readily today in their social roles.

Until the modern age, sexual power and force over the other was more acceptable. Men functioned with a double standard (polygamy and serial divorce were permitted in the Hebrew Bible). In marriage, men set the sexual norms. A man might take a concubine if his wife could not conceive; a married man did not commit adultery if he had sex with a single woman; a widow had to have sex with her brother-in-law if her husband died childless. In some parts of the world, a woman killed herself when her husband pre-deceased her. Even today, female circumcision and the social confinement of women victimize women.

Our problems with sexuality today are not trivial but they may be less dreadful than those of the past we have cited. Reproductive rights are asserted but they are balanced by a mutuality and equity which are new in human affairs and are welcome.

Abortion and contraception have been more readily utilized in our day but it is important to evaluate these choices in proper historical context.

Throughout the pagan world and all through the centuries of Christian European culture, unwanted children were abandoned in great numbers. Indeed, there were places assigned in the Roman Forum and, later, designated monasteries where children were forsaken, anonymously, by distressed mothers. Often these children were taken up by those, even monks, who sexually abused them or exploited them for profit.

In 1198, Pope Innocent III opened the first foundling home when fishermen informed him that their nets regularly retrieved from the Tiber River the bodies of drowned infants. Without the resources to care for their children and without reproductive choices or remedies, many parents left their children to die.

Without effective contraception, people had more children than their resources allowed. In any case, reproductive rights for the individual and mutuality in sexual experience are positive developments and represent ethical progress.

## Conclusion

Religion is more effective with sexual ethics when it is less specific (as Jesus was in the Gospel). Pastoral care brings sexual crises to resolution less violently and harshly than institutional mandates which preempt this care and force it into unhelpful categories. There are times when divorce is a moral imperative and times when it is simply destructive.

There are times when contraception is essential to responsible parenting and times when it is intrinsically selfish. The list can be expanded but the point is obvious. Pastoral care needs to function under broad guidelines, with fewer specifics and warnings.

Sexual norms, formulated by institutions, are frequently self-serving, politically charged, and monarchically promulgated.

Allow me to conclude with a note about religion and Church.

People do not join Churches today to be defined by them. They enlist because they sense the transcendent in their lives and need relief from an exclusively utilitarian world. They do not seek sexual guidance but social contact and community. They are not moved by the specificity of creeds or ethical systems. Indeed conservative Christians are frequently no different from liberal Christians in their sexual behavior and in the number of official Church policies they selectively ignore.

Fulminations against abortion and contraception have not kept Catholics, in large numbers, from resorting to both in the same percentages that hold for the general population. And Catholics who choose these options continue to see themselves as Catholics and to take communion.

Today, people turn to the Churches to address the mystery in their lives, to cope with suffering and death, to find a hope the world at large does not always give. Religion and the Church ought not to be total monarchical systems in which all is determined in advance and unilaterally. Democracies, on the contrary, are elective systems to the extent this is compatible with social order and human rights. People now seek the Churches as elective and, as it were, democratic systems.

This does not make the Church less dear. Do people in democracies love their nation less?

Does the Church one chooses with all one's heart not become an object of love nonetheless, perhaps even more ardently than the Church one is compelled to serve? Does choosing one's wife or husband make that person less valuable than when others make the choice?

It is time for us to see power and sex in a new light for the sake of the Church and for the sake of the Gospel which proclaims a Christ who rejects power far more rigorously than sexual misdeeds.

# Chapter Five
# The Parliament of World Religions

When diversity seeks community, the human heart is enriched. When the world's religions search for common ground, the human spirit is enlarged.

We shall consider the first four Parliaments of the World Religions. These set the model for all future assemblies.

The parliaments began in America in Chicago in 1893, slightly more than a century after the 1791 ratification of the United States Constitution's Bill of Rights.

The democratic instinct of forging unity from diversity helped generate a parliament in the United States where religions would meet on equal terms. Indeed, it was precisely American secularity, permitting all religions a voice but giving no religion a preference, which made the United States a fitting environment for this new experiment. And, so, in 1893 (September 11-28), the first Parliament convened, in Chicago, with some 7,000 people. Buddhists, Jews, Christians, Confucians, and Hindus were present. Invitations did not go out to Muslims, Native Americans, or Sikhs. Frederick Douglass was present at this historic meeting as he was in 1848 at Seneca Falls, the assembly inaugurating the women's rights movement.

The first Parliament was significant in its very occurrence. Its greatest accomplishment was its act of existence.

## The Second Parliament

There was not a second Parliament until 1993 (August 28-September 5), a century later, again in Chicago. Developments toward unity in many areas made the Parliament of an earlier age seem less exotic. The twentieth century put in place the World Council of Churches, the United Nations, the Universal Declaration of Human Rights, Vatican II, the European Union, the globalization of telecommunication and travel. The 1993 Parliament gathered 8,000 delegates. It differed from the 1893 assembly in important ways:

- Inclusivity: no religious group was excluded
- Suitability: the emerging global context made universal religious dialogue desirable and imperative
- Testimony: the "Declaration Toward a Global Ethic" was adopted

The Parliament was profoundly influenced by the Dalai Lama whose good offices and personal credibility gave the Parliament a second birth. Hans Kung, fusing clarity, practicality and profundity, focused the attention of the Parliament on a global ethic. The Declaration was a worthy companion for the Universal Declaration of Human Rights and might never have emerged without it. It stresses responsibilities to accompany human rights.

The world's religions find ethical imperatives in the human heart and in their sacred texts and institutional memories. Religions endorse two general principles and hold in common four moral guidelines.

The general principles:

- Human beings must be dealt with humanely
- We must do to others only what we would want done to ourselves

The guidelines:

- Life must be respected (no killing)
- Property must be respected (no stealing)
- Truth must be respected (no lying)
- Sexual life must be respected (no exploitation)

Respect for life is linked with respect for the planet and its ecology. Respect for property is contiguous with social justice. Respect for truth reforms political and religious systems. Respect for sexual life develops into reproductive rights and gender equality. The first Parliament showed that world religions can gather in effective dialogue. The second Parliament proved that religious traditions can achieve ethical consensus and issue a common document.

## THE THIRD PARLIAMENT

On the eve of the third millennium in Africa where human life emerged, the third Parliament met from December 1-8, 1999. Seven thousand delegates from 90 countries came to Cape Town, South Africa where Nelson Mandela addressed the assembly. Like Gandhi, Mandela fused politics and religion, non-violence and resistance, suffering and compassion. Neither man was perfect or beyond fault but each was sufficiently credible to galvanize and unify people across an extraordinary range of diversity. The Dalai Lama again was the strong and gentle presence giving the Parliament continuity, stability and hope. The Dalai Lama and Nelson Mandela, both Nobel Peace laureates, embodied respectively a religious tradition and a political entity.

Yet, the Dalai Lama spoke of political action, warning delegates not to dissipate their energy in prayer and meditation when action on behalf of others was required. Mandela, conversely, referred to religion, claiming it "was one of the motivating factors in bringing down apartheid" and, indeed, enabling him to reject cynicism and become politically and personally what he was now. Mandela cancelled a trip to Washington D.C. so that he might address the Parliament.

Ela Gandhi, granddaughter of Mahatma Gandhi, on stage with the Dalai Lama and Nelson Mandela, formed a mosaic of hope uniting Hindu, Buddhist, and Christian believers. She, a member of her country's governing parliament, represented as well the relationship of politics and religion.

The 1993 Parliament focused on a global ethic, as we have seen. The 1999 Parliament drafted an Earth Charter stressing ecological theology. It presents peace as the product of a new relationship with the earth as well as with the human family. The Charter calls for "reverence for the mystery of being, gratitude for the gift of life, and humility regarding the human place in nature."

The 1999 Parliament described its mission in broad terms:

- The Parliament seeks harmony, not unity
- It is about convergence, not consensus
- It intends creative engagement, not structure

Hans Kung crafted the organizing theme for the entire parliamentary experience:

- No peace among the nations without peace among the religions
- No peace among the religions without dialogue between the religions

In the midst of the color and drama, the music and meditation, the exhibits and rituals, there was present a unifying conviction that religions are permanent institutions and, collectively, have an enormous potential to improve the world. Religions may be our most enduring structures and our most expansive organizations, embracing virtually the whole of humanity.

There is a resistance to define exactly what a religion is but a sense that the transcendent, however named or encountered, grounds our sense of the sacred and shapes what we call religion.

**PARLIAMENT 2004**

For the first time, the Parliament, conceived and developed in the United States and brought to new maturity in Africa, came to Europe. This was the first Parliament summoned on the five-year schedule that will now make Parliaments chronologically predictable. It was scheduled for Barcelona. Spain was the country from which Columbus sailed for Europe's encounter with half of the globe it did not realize existed. Barcelona is the city where Picasso was formed as a painter, the place where Antoni Gaudi gave architecture one of the most awesome buildings ever created, the Sagrada Familia.

In the interval between the parliaments, a Museum of World Religions was opened (2001) on the Asian continent in Taipei, Taiwan. This massive, eight thousand square meter building, a decade in development, is replete with art and a library, music and theater space, seminar and meditation rooms.

One hundred and eleven years after the first Parliament, some 7,700 delegates, large numbers of them quite young, arrived from 75 countries. In little more than a decade since its 1993 rebirth, the Parliament assembled three meetings, established its center of operations in Chicago, witnessed the creation of a museum of world religions, and crafted a Global Ethic and Earth Charter.

## Religious Violence

A less promising awareness was the level of incendiary religious violence since the last parliament. The trauma of 9/11 in New York City and Madrid's Atocha train tragedy of March 11, the Iraq war, and the Israeli-Palestinian conflict, the Sudan and, not so long ago, ethnic cleansing in the former Yugoslavia, in Sri Lanka and Ruwanda,—all this horror and more was inflamed by the misguided use of religious language and symbols.

Reflective reports at the Parliament questioned whether religious sacrifices in blood rituals predispose people toward violence. Unfortunately, all sacred texts provide an opportunity to justify violence. The interpretation of these texts is only as moral as the reader and the group that receive them. If a community stresses a violent understanding of its tradition, an entire religious system resorts to darkness and death.

Virtually all religions allow violence under certain conditions. The conditions are the troubling element. Yet the institutions for nonviolence do not seem sufficiently developed to keep the world safe and free.

The World Council of Churches, struggling with this dilemma, reached an ambiguous conclusion:

- Nonviolent action is the ideal
- In extreme situations, a just war may be a necessity
- Violence is unavoidable where nonviolence is inadequate

Nonetheless, the religious legitimization of violence does not occur in a historical vacuum. The Parliament focus on water, debt, and refugees makes this clear. Graham Fuller recently remarked in Foreign Affairs: "If society and its politics are violent and unhappy, its mode of religious expression is likely to be just the same." Furthermore, one must not be naïve about the fact that state-sponsored violence is far worse than religious violence. The degraded social environment and even state violence, however, cannot excuse religious violence. They do, however, give us a context to understand this violence and a sense that these other abnormalities must be addressed as we seek a total solution to religious violence.

Diana Eck of Harvard University observes that religions which are exclusivist have the potential of being the most dangerous. She divides religious systems along three lines:

- Exclusivist: one religious system is true, all others false
- Inclusivist: many religious systems are good but one is better
- Pluralist: religious systems are different in equally valid ways

One of the most vexing problems in addressing religious violence is determining the proper relationship between secular states and religious institutions. Theocracies give too much power to religion and are prone to violence. Obsessive atheistic states, on the other hand, take too much power to themselves and become persecutors. Some moderate accommodations also have serious liabilities:

- A partly secular state with one religion allowed to dominate

- A fully secular state with religion totally privatized

The best solution seems to call for a secular state where religions are invited to play an important role in influencing public policy through a democratic process. This does not ensure harmony, but it does allow different players a proper role.

In this arrangement, the secular state is free to conduct the political business of the nation, limited by democracy, an autonomous judicial system, and a free press. Religions are free to define their legitimacy within the context of civil law and human rights. They are free to proclaim the insufficiency of purely secular and political definitions of life, free to serve the state's citizens in their search for transcendent connections as well as cosmic and personal meanings.

Martin Luther King may have expressed the issue of violence best:

> "Returning violence for violence multiplies violence adding deeper darkness to a night already devoid of stars. Darkness cannot drive out darkness; only light can do that. Hate cannot drive out hate; only love can do that."

## Intra-religious Dialogue

The model for dialogues at the Parliament was intra-religious and inter-religious. There is no meaningful way to synthesize an event that includes a thousand lectures and seminars catalogued in a program of 259 pages.

A sense of how delegates debated issues may be gathered from considering one intra-religious discussion and one inter-religious discussion.

Since Christianity is the largest religious institution, we might consider how some of its theologians, leaders, and delegates are thinking.

How can a religion as exclusivist as Christianity meet the challenge of dialogue with world religions?

One approach is to emphasize experience over doctrine, lived encounters over institutional priorities. There are examples from history which show this approach.

In the first century, Christianity radically redefined itself, moving away from the strictly Jewish categories of Jesus and the Twelve to the Greco-Roman experiences of later Christians. No longer were circumcision or Torah, Sabbath or Temple, priesthood and sacrifice, Passover and the holy days required. These were not incidental or marginal matters but went to the essence of how Christians first defined themselves. Christianity accommodated itself to the changed experience of its adherents. It found a way to connect this with its prior tradition, but it did so by bringing in doctrines and believers who would not have been accepted in an earlier age.

Another, less radical example is the Second Vatican Council. Catholicism redefined its teaching on ecumenism and inter-religious dialogue, on the celebration of liturgy and the role of the laity, on the priority of Scripture over later Church teaching, on marriage and sexual norms, on collegial structures of authority and other substantial matters. The heresy of a former time became the doctrine of a later generation.

Substantial dialogue with other religions may necessitate new reflection on the nature of God and the identity of Christ. Christianity once defined monotheism in a way that allowed a plurality of divine persons. This looked like polytheism to many Jews, and, later, Muslims. Christian conceptions of divinity are cast in Greco-Roman categories and philosophy. We might ask whether Christianity's creative approach to defining God is finished. Are there new possibilities which the experience of inter-religious dialogue many reveal?

We must ask, on another issue, whether the link between Christ and salvation has been correctly formulated. If Christ is savior, how should this be defined? Is Christ part of a much larger salvation system, a system incomplete without him but a system which finds adequate place for revelation and grace in other religions?

The Second Vatican Council maintained that the other Christian Churches mediate salvation to their believing members. That statement would have taken away the breath of more orthodox Catholics a generation earlier. Might it not be true that religions minister salvation to their believing members in ways we have not adequately addressed?

Salvation is a broad category in the Bible, so broad that all creation is said to be saved. How concretely is this true if so much of creation does not, and did not, and will not, affirm Christ?

Will this thinking endanger commitment to God or Christ? We might ask if Catholics think less of Catholicism when they value Protestantism more. Do people love their own mothers less when they appreciate more expansively the lives of other mothers?

## Inter-religious Discussion

Not surprisingly, the inter-religious discussion moved in every way imaginable across the spectrum of global concerns and Parliament workshops.

The figure of Mahatma Gandhi served as a synthesizing model or symbol for all the discussions in their diverse developments.

Indeed, Gandhi, the Dalai Lama, and Nelson Mandela may be the most abiding icons or unifying images for all the Parliaments thus far. Martin Luther King may also serve as an impressive influence, but his work has been less cited by the Parliament than the other three.

What were, then, some of the ways Gandhi was presented at the 2004 Parliament? One of the recurring themes was the ease with which Gandhi identified with the world's religions and found enlightenment in them.

As a law student in London, Gandhi studied Buddhist, Christian, Hindu, and Jain literature in a search for God and truth. He read the Bhagavad Gita every day. Later, the Qur'an was part of his daily reading.

Ela Gandhi, his granddaughter, tells of an early experience Gandhi had at the Catholic Cistercian monastery some thirty kilometers from Durban, South Africa. He learned there lessons which helped him form his first ashram, in South Africa, in 1904:

- Monks, nuns, students worked equally in manual labor
- Races and genders were equally part of the community
- All work was equally valued from cleaning bathrooms to writing

At the first ashram Gandhi allowed no privileged place for a particular religious service. One prayed, whatever one's denomination, outside, under the sky. Gandhi observed:

> " . . . after long study and experience, I have come to the conclusion that all religions are true; all religions have some error in them; all religions are almost as dear to me as my own Hinduism . . ."

Gandhi asked himself three key questions in assessing authentic religious commitment:

- What, indeed, is your religion?
- How have you been led to this religion?
- What bearing does this religion have on personal behavior and social justice?

The second and third questions are pivotal.

Gandhi came to realize, in answering the second question, that it is not helpful to proclaim that "God is Truth." A better formulation: "Truth is God." We can deny God, but we do not deny the value of truth.

The search for truth does not lead one away from reason or from the testimony of other, even contrary voices. Religious leaders must not hide dishonestly behind their own images and frailties, pretending to be what they are not. For Gandhi, then, it must be truth which leads to religion and to God, to dialogue with others and to religious leadership.

The third question considers the relationship of religion to one's social justice agenda. Religion intends the transformation of the inner self but this must extend to the social order.

One could not be leading a truly religious life unless this connected with the whole of humanity. This happens impressively by taking part in politics.

Gandhi's commitment to religion and politics leads him to create a list of seven deadly social sins:

- Wealth without work
- Pleasure without conscience
- Knowledge without character
- Commerce without morality
- Science without humanity
- Worship without sacrifice
- Politics without principle

In choosing to work for social justice, Gandhi observes that the world has enough to satisfy our need but not our greed. As the Parliament centers on water, debt, and refugees, it is helpful to realize we are not without resources but we lack the will to distribute them equitably.

Gandhi ties together the essential themes of the Parliament: finding the sacred in other religions and in the human heart; moving from religious commitment to political process and social justice; struggling for social justice non-violently.

Gandhi adds,however, that the struggle for justice in civil disobedience and even in nonviolence is not as demanding as the imperative to act in love. Love is the ultimate achievement of all authentic religion and the only abiding value in a reformed political system and social order.

Gandhi manages, in one life, to give expression to the major themes of inter-religious dialogue.

## EPILOGUE

Inter-religious dialogue begins with a sense that other religions have values that one's own religion has not realized. It proceeds on the conviction that the humanity we share and the planet we inhabit make us members of the same family.

As members of the same family we search for common ground and a common language. The Parliament met twice in five years. In Cape Town, in 1999, we were given an enduring image of hope as the Dalai Lama, a Buddhist, Nelson Mandela, a Christian, and Ela Gandhi, a Hindu, shared a common stage one night and galvanized 7000 delegates in a tidal wave of gratitude and hope. In Barcelona, in 2004, a second indelible image was created. Before one of the world's most awesome buildings, the Sagrada Familia of Antoni Gaudi, lights and color, costume and dance, music and chant expressed the grace and beauty religions inspire.

No word has been heard more often than the word "peace" at Parliamentary assemblies over the years. This ancient dream and present hope have never been far from the human heart.

We speak of peace so often because without it we have no future worth living.

# SECTION THREE

## Becoming Faithful and Self-Defined

# Chapter Six
# Hearing the Voice of the Faithful

## The Beginning

Luke tells us how it all began. He liked to do this. He begins the story of Jesus with the conception, the only evangelist to do so. In Acts, he gives us the conception, as it were, of the Christian Community, on Pentecost, and this also by the Spirit.

Luke writes that the community, not just the apostles, are gathered: "all of them in one place." He adds: "all of them were filled with the Holy Spirit" and, indeed "all of them began to speak in other languages as the Spirit gave them ability" (Acts 2). Luke has Peter declare that your sons and your daughters are prophets; today, your young men see visions and your old men dream dreams.

The Church is born as a community. All are given the Spirit; all preach; all see; all have visions and dreams. It is Pentecost.

Two millennia later, in our era, Vatican II, the first Council in Church history to deal with the laity as a structure of the Church, captures this Pentecost theme. It teaches that Tradition and Scripture were entrusted to the "practice and life of the believing . . . church," not solely to the episcopal magisterium. The community determines which books make up the New Testament, what they mean, and how they can be brought to life in the Church (*Dei Verbum*, 8).

The marks or signs of the Catholic Church are found in the community, derived from the Spirit, of course, but made visible by the community. The community makes the Church one, holy, catholic, and apostolic.

The gathering of the faithful makes the Church one. Baptism unites the Church, not ordination.

The faithful make the Church holy, through, what Vatican II called, its practice of the faith and its spirituality (*Dei Verbum* 8).

Without the faithful dispersed through the world, the Church is not catholic or universal.

Indeed, the Church is apostolic because the community accepts the Christ the apostles and the apostolic age proclaimed. This apostolic faith has its origins, not only in the Twelve, but in the women at the cross and the disciples who buried Jesus, and the Easter faith of Magdalene. The acceptance of faith by the Twelve certainly matters, but Pentecost celebrates the fact that the Twelve chosen by Jesus have become a larger community, commissioned by Christ in the Spirit. Apostolicity refers to a period in the Church's life, not to the Twelve alone. No one in the first century feared the Church would die when the Twelve died. The larger Church had received Pentecost and the Spirit and the dreams and the visions. The New Testament is clear about this.

Without the community at large, the Church cannot be one, holy, catholic and apostolic. Period.

Eastern Christianity understood the link between baptism and the community better than Western Christianity did; Christianity, in the West, is only a partial Church without the East and vice versa. John Paul II reminded us that the Church has only one lung without the East. We can conclude from this that the breath of the Spirit does not breathe fully in the body of the Church if it is received with only one lung.

In the West, in the fifth century, baptism was linked, by Augustine, to original sin. Augustine was brilliant beyond description. But he got this wrong. In the East, where Christianity began and where all the Councils of the first millennium were held, the focus in baptism was on becoming the People of God.

The Church learns, early in its history, that the Spirit is best discerned in community, in councils, in synods. The Church learns also that the Spirit is revealed in the history of the People of God. It is not given all at once. Jesus at the Last Supper told us this. There were other lessons, he observed, that could not be received now, all in one moment.

Thus, the acceptance of the Gentiles was not credible to the Church in the year 35 and yet became doctrine in the year 50 at the Jerusalem Council.

In our era, we have seen that women priests were not a credible option for the community a century ago and seem to be an imperative now; ecumenism was unthinkable for Catholics at large in 1865 and became conciliar teaching in 1965; a lay-led Communion Service was prohibited in 1935 and promoted in 1995.

What made the difference? The community and its experience with Gentiles or women or Protestants or enlightened laity. The Spirit led the community to accept what Church administrators once denounced. The norm through Church history has been this: Church administrators follow what the community at large accepts. Church administrators matter but never as much as the community does.

We were told: "when two or three are gathered in my name, I am among them" (Matthew 18: 20). Notice there is no hierarchy in that number. We were taught:

> You know that the rulers of the Gentiles lord it over them and their great ones are tyrants over them. It will not be so among you but, whoever wishes to be great among you must be your servant . . . (Matthew 20: 25-26).

Is this not clear?

Then how did we miss it?

## The Community and Doctrine

There are three magisterial or teaching structures in the Church: episcopal (papal), theological, communitarian. Teaching is formally expressed by the episcopal magisterium. This teaching is not authentic and cannot be considered infallible unless a genuine dialogue among bishops and theologians and the community at large is a substantial part of it.

John Henry Newman, in his classic 1859 document, "On Consulting the Faithful in Matters of Doctrine" said it well: " . . . the body of the faithful . . . and their consensus is the voice of the Infallible Church. . . ."

The chronological order in which the Church understands its faith is, first, *sensus fidelium*. This *sensus* is the response the community makes to whatever it receives. From this response, Tradition emerges. These unwritten resources guide the Church for the first few centuries, including, of course, the apostolic age. Eventually, both of them lead to the written Scripture, which comes last.

What this Scripture is, which books make it up, and what they mean depend upon the *sensus fidelium* and Tradition. Scripture emerges in the Church from the community at large; there is no record anywhere that it came about after a meeting of Church administrators or in any other way. Scripture becomes the privileged expression of this faith, a faith already there. It is, then, not a text-book written by a few but a communal endeavor developed by all.

Around the year 70, or relatively soon after, the original apostles who knew the pre-Easter Jesus have died. Except for the seven authentic Pauline letters, most of the New Testament is written after their death. Gospels do not appeal to the Twelve for their authority or as a guide to what constitutes the New Testament.

The community is inspired to receive Scripture. Scripture is not accepted because it is inspired; it is inspired because it is accepted. The authority of an apostle means less than the community acceptance of a doctrine.

Following Newman's lead, a doctrine not received is not infallible. Infallibility in teaching depends on infallibility in believing and receiving, not the other way around.

Furthermore, doctrine in the Church does not have as its object the proclamation of a truth. Its intent is pastoral care, spirituality, an encounter with God. What is said is less important than the effect it has on people.

Thomas Aquinas tells us that faith reaches for the reality beyond the doctrine, God, for example, who cannot be put into words (S.T. 2; 2q.1). We know from our own experience, that how we say we love someone is less important than the love we seek to express and the willingness of another to receive the love. This does not mean that the words have no value, but that the love matters more and the reception by the other matters most.

This consensus of the faithful is never valid if it is forced. In a totalitarian system, force is a factor in creating compliance. In a believing community, agreement must be free. The believing community is now freely at work in receiving Vatican II and determining how it is accepted. The community has affirmed the major themes of that Council: collegiality, liturgical and biblical renewal, ecumenism, religious freedom, and conscience. The turbulence of the last fifty years is not caused by resistance to the Council by people, but by their desire to implement the Council and to do this even while Church administrators resist their efforts. The turbulence shows us people coming to terms with the Council and making it work.

Let us apply the norms for reception to the papacy. It is not the election of a pope that makes a pope legitimate, but the acceptance of that election by people. Many elected popes were not accepted and anti-popes or multiple popes emerged. The Council of Constance (1414-1417) was an assembly of the community in the name of the Spirit. It led to the removal of all three current popes and the election of a new pope who could be accepted throughout Christianity. When popes fail, the community rescues the Church. This is not theory; it is history.

The pope does not unify or sanctify the Church and does not make it catholic or apostolic. This is the work of the Spirit and the community. The pope is an institutional sign of a unity already achieved by the faithful. The pope does not create a community of believers or validate baptisms or make the Eucharist occur.

Let us go further. In Church doctrine and law, all the laity are empowered to baptize. This baptism makes every recipient a member of the Church. The faithful who make visible the four marks of the Church are not only so-called practicing Catholics. Indeed, Vatican II never limits the faithful to those practicing Catholicism in a certain way.

Part of the reason for this is that it is difficult to define a practicing Catholic. Those who participate regularly in the sacraments may be blind to the Gospel message of justice and the beatitudes. Sometimes the holy are simply ignorant, as Teresa of Avila reminds us.

Does the Spirit abandon those who, for good reasons, no longer attend

Sunday Eucharist regularly? If these so-called non-practicing Catholics serve the disadvantaged or raise their families with Gospel values or become martyrs in their ministry to the marginalized, are they not practicing Catholics? What do we say, furthermore, about the witness of other Christians, also baptized, in Orthodox and Protestant churches? Is it not facile to dismiss them from the *sensus fidelium*? Does this not become all the more difficult to do when Jesus, we know, was open to the religiously alienated and even encouraged marginality?

We must be sensitive not to the tidiness Church administrators may prefer but to the diverse ways the baptized live out their faith, make sense of their lives and follow the charisms and conscience the Spirit gives them, especially when the institutional Church fails them.

The *sensus fidelium* is evaluated less in terms of its consistency with institutional orthodoxy and more in terms of the Gospel. Indeed, when an institution is enamored of its own orthodoxy, it dismisses not only so-called non-practicing Catholics but also practicing Catholics when they are not servile. Many practicing Catholics have reached a different consensus on birth control and a married priesthood and are not taken into account by Church administrators.

There are two other issues to address before we conclude this section.

The first of these is how we discern the *sensus fidelium*. This is more difficult to gauge than the consensus of bishops or theologians, because the field is so large.

There are many ways to do this, however, if there is good will on the part of the hierarchy, in discerning the faith and life of the larger community. Let us cite seven of these:

- Parish and diocesan councils, free of intimidation or interference

- Councils or senates of priests in charge of their own affairs

- Chapters of women and men religious inspired by the charism of their calling
- Catholic reform and renewal organizations of regional, national, and international standing
- Public and inclusive consultation in drafting pastoral letters
- Ecumenical and inter-religious dialogues and assemblies
- Polls and surveys professionally and respectfully conducted

In any case, we never articulate a truth absolutely, free of all conditions of time and language. Never. The *sensus fidelium* may receive a doctrine in one era and reject it in another, not because the faithful are frivolous but because they sense the emergence of new circumstances, often before Church administrators do. Thus, mandatory celibacy may make sense in one century but not another. The restriction of ordination to men may have a point in one culture but not in another. Birth control may express different values in one set of circumstances but not another. Separation of Church and State may not work in one era but become imperative as societies include greater diversity and heterogeneity.

John Henry Newman reminded us that truth is "the daughter of time" (*Development of Christian Doctrine*, Notre Dame Press, 1989). Time gives us the experience to see deeper into a truth and to adjust our understanding of it.

The last issue in this section focuses on what the *sensus fidelium* adds to the magisterium of the bishops or the theologians that they cannot achieve without it.

The *sensus fidelium* is more directly incarnational and concrete, more calibrated to daily living, more attuned to how a teaching is lived out in the realities of marriage and family, career, and civic life. The *sensus fidelium* makes a teaching catholic and rejects it when it is not resilient enough to be universal. Church administrators may live in a single culture, Roman or European, or in a single class system, clerical or curial, and become impervious to knowing how or whether this doctrine, albeit impressive in formulation, works outside the narrow framework of its construction.

Without recourse to the *sensus fidelium*, Church administrators may lose the value of a more inclusive sensibility of faith, one that stresses relationality over uniformity. Some issues elude a single-stated standard: end of life care for a loved one; the same-sex marriage of a son or daughter; offering Protestant Christians sacraments; deciding when artificial birth control may become a moral imperative; calling a sexually abusive priest or bishop to Christian responsibility.

Without a *sensus fidelium*, we lose dimensions of our humanity and we expose the Gospel and the very faith we cherish to suffocating conformities where the Spirit cannot breathe and where both lungs of the Church struggle for life and are not able to function.

## The Community and Law

We begin this section with eight assumptions about authority and law that Church administrators and people at large accept, at least in principle. Church administrators, indeed, the Vatican, would not want to go on public record rejecting any one of these:

- There is a true equality among the baptized
- Authority intends the good of community and not its own advantage
- The papacy and canon law exist for the good of the Church at large
- A responsible lawmaker does not create law to burden the community
- Legitimate authority seeks to be credible and effective

- No church officer promotes isolation from the community

- It is dangerous to ignore massive resistance to a law even if that resistance is wrong

- Church officers want a culture of dialogue in some measure and have set up structures to facilitate this

Let us see how these assumptions affect law and the way we live in the Church. We note that law in the Church is law only by analogy. It is different from secular law. It is much closer to theology than to jurisprudence. Its intent is spirituality rather than compliance. This is why the last canon, 1752, reads:

> "The salvation of souls . . . is always the supreme law of the Church."

In the Church, law is not valid unless it is accepted by the community. This principle goes back sixteen centuries, to Augustine. It is written into the first codification of canon law by Gratian, in the twelfth century. Indeed, an intelligent, responsible interpretation by the community makes the law better and enhances the authority of the legislator.

Secular law is valid as formulated if the proper procedure has been followed. Church law is invalid, even if proper procedure has been followed, if the community does not accept it. Even if the law has been received by the Church at large, a local community of Christians may decide it does not apply to them. They are free then, under law, to create a contrary custom. This contrary custom becomes the law if it continues for thirty years without a formal reaction from the lawmaker. The contrary custom creates in itself a new law. A bishop, therefore, not answering mail, as many do not, actually contributes to the development of contrary custom. Silence is the same as agreement in canon law.

In all of this, we must avoid two extremes: robotic obedience to law with no discernment and, absolutely elective behavior in which we do anything we want. In any case, we are explicitly told in Canon Law that "Custom is the best interpreter of laws" (Canon 27). Custom, therefore, matters more than judicial review by those who know the law or scholarship by those who have researched it. Custom supercedes every other way of dealing with the law. It comes from the instinct and sense of the People of God.

A further restriction on law in the Church is called *epikeia*. It applies even to an individual. A group or a single person may conclude that the specific circumstances of their life were not taken into account in the law. The law, therefore, does not apply to them. This is derived from the eight assumptions we have specified. The lawmaker never intends to burden needlessly or to harm the community or individual. We take for granted that we are all acting in good faith.

The Church, we see, officially allows lawlessness. It makes clear that breaking a Church law may be illegal but it is legitimate. After thirty years of resistance, with no formal response from a lawmaker, the resistance becomes legal, as we have seen.

There are a number of times when this resistance prevailed:

- The Eastern Catholic Church refused to accept mandatory celibacy.
- The 1917 Code of Canon Law required every diocese to have a synod every ten years; bishops, including the Bishop of Rome, did not comply.
- John XXIII decreed in *Veterum Sapientia* (1962) that all seminaries in the world must conduct all theological lectures in Latin. Professors around the world assumed the directive did not apply to them because they did not know Latin well and had not the time to learn it properly or, if they did, their students would not understand it; Rome allowed the contrary custom to prevail.
- Fasting for a time before receiving communion is ignored.

- Communion is given, at the discretion of the minister, to divorced and remarried Catholics and to homosexual couples. John Paul II gave communion to Prime Minister Tony Blair in the Vatican, when he was an Anglican.

- Communion is received regularly by Catholics who attend Protestant worship services.

- Catholic couples often live together before a Church wedding.

- Limbo was doubted and denied for centuries until it was recently rejected by the pope.

- When eating meat on Friday was prohibited, Catholic countries in Europe simply did not comply and the law was changed.

- The obligation to attend Sunday Mass, or go to confession, is reinterpreted by Catholics to take into account their individual circumstances.

The power or authority of the lawgiver is not a sufficient norm in Catholic law and theology. Good law is meant to bring peace to the community. Therefore, canon law is obliged to look to the community to judge if this is happening and to act accordingly when it is not. There is a noteworthy difference between the 1917 Code of Canon Law in which the People of God are not given priority and the 1983 Code in which they are. The difference is due to Vatican II. The response of the People of God to the law, therefore, must be encouraged, not distrusted.

It should be clear by now that the *sensus fidelium* is the point of convergence in Catholic life for law, reception, community, conscience, and faith.

The escalating division in the Catholic Church between what people believe and what administrators teach, between how people behave and what lawmakers require is not due solely to secularism or self-indulgence. Educated and autonomous Catholics do not accept monarchical legislation.

They force a culture of dialogue on the Church by non-compliance if they have not been consulted or taken into account.

The three magisterial or teaching offices in the Church (bishops, theologians, and the People of God) are obliged by Church teaching to create a culture of dialogue between and among them. If this does not happen, the community acts accordingly. Today, bishops at large ignore university scholarship and have contempt for the *sensus fidelium* when it is not compliant. The response of people has been active and passive resistance to being governed in such a manner.

This crisis gives us the opportunity to act creatively and responsibly. Two examples of creative resistance or reinterpretation are intentional communities and appropriate definitions of what it means to be Catholic. These two examples show the community using its own sense of things on the doctrinal level and on the level of law.

**First, intentional communities.**

Large numbers of people in the United States have abandoned parishes, often with sadness, when these parishes seem to have lost the Gospel or, even, basic human decency and polite behavior.

Three-quarters of Catholics no longer attend Sunday Liturgy regularly. It is difficult to believe that three-quarters of the Catholic population are simply misguided. It is dangerous to dismiss massive resistance. More to the point, many of these believers still have sacramental and spiritual needs.

The intentional community is one response to these needs. These communities carry the liability of including only the like-minded, but parishes are not immune from this either. Intentional communities may, unintentionally, limit public access but parishes also do this when they treat people disrespectfully and celebrate liturgies which cater excessively to those who are reactionary and very judgmental.

The new Code of Canon Law (1983), for the first time in history, gives people a right of association.

> "The Christian faithful are at liberty freely to found and govern associations for charitable or religious purposes . . . they are free to hold meetings to pursue these purposes in common (Canon 215)."

This, my friends, is a Bill of Rights for intentional communities, *de jure* and *de facto.* It is a charter for VOTF and for the American Catholic Council as well.

The next canon gives Catholics the right to take the initiative in apostolic actions on their own behalf.

> "All the Catholic faithful, since they participate in the mission of the Church, have the right to promote or to sustain apostolic action by their own undertakings . . . (Canon 216)."

Intentional communities gain increased legitimacy in direct proportion to the lack of credibility and pastoral care in Catholic parishes. Catholics have the right to respond to the plundering of their parishes by acting on their own behalf. There is a true equality among the baptized. Authority, remember, intends the good of the community. A responsible lawmaker does not create law to burden the community.

These words are not rhetoric. They are pastoral imperatives and law for the Church.

**The second creative initiative is an appropriate definition of what it means to be Catholic.**

We begin by observing that only baptism is necessary for Church membership. Belief and obedience are not required in Church law or teaching for membership. Otherwise, many bishops would no longer be Catholics. No bishop or pope has the right to determine who is a member of the Church. If this were so, we would have a bishops' Church and not Christ's Church.

Membership is determined by baptism. Period. This membership is permanent and cannot be revoked by a bishop or the pope.

The official Church confirms this by including as Catholics all those baptized as Catholics. This is very different from the way Protestant churches count their members. Catholic baptism holds for membership even if one does nothing Catholic after baptism. I offer one example of how the official Church confirms this by its own actions. Church law requires that a baptized Catholic be married in a Catholic ceremony, even if that baptized Catholic never did anything Catholic after baptism.

How then does one know if one is Catholic? Baptism suffices but there are other convincing signs, many of which apply to the vast majority of Catholics here.

- A sense of belonging or being at home in the Catholic Church, broadly defined
- A love of Christ, the New Testament, the Eucharist
- An awareness that Catholicism helps me to make sense of my life
- A conviction that I have been called to be Catholic
- A recognition by Catholics at large that I am a Catholic
- A deep respect for the *sensus fidelium*
- A commitment to Vatican II

If these categories do not fit, it is enough that you have been baptized Catholic.

Catholicism is not measured by compliance with present Church policy, in fact or by law. That is too narrow a definition, too uncatholic, if you will. If such a criterion were strictly applied, Francis Assisi, Thomas Aquinas, and John Henry Newman were not Catholics. Nor were those nineteenth-century dissidents Catholic when they rejected Pius IX's call for armed conflict and violence to defend the Papal States with bloodshed against the invading Italian forces. Nor were the early-twentieth-century liturgical reformers calling for the liturgy later endorsed by Vatican II. Nor were the condemned biblical scholars seeking a critical interpretation of the New Testament, until Vatican II itself went in their direction.

We must not measure Catholicism by something as transient as current Church policy or as restrictive as how the very docile receive official directives. Creative disaffiliation matters immensely for the spiritual good of the Church. Subversive wisdom requires that we indict nonsense, especially when it poses as intelligence. When Church administrators are blind, there must be room for prophets and for those who read the signs of the times and not only *L'Osservatore Romano*.

In any case, Church authority cannot be authentic unless and until the community validates it.

One of my favorite Jesuit authors, a professor of mine at the Gregorian University in Rome, said it well:

> "Authority is the quality of leadership which elicits and justifies the willingness ... to be led ("Authority in an Ecclesiology of Communion," Francis Sullivan, *New Theological Review* 10, 1997, 18-30)."

With even greater authority Vatican II's Constitution on the Church tells us:

> "The universal body of the faithful ... cannot be mistaken in believing ... (12)."

## Apostolic Imagination

A Latin saying encapsulates this section succinctly:

> "*Ecclesia est semper ipse sed numquam idem*
> (The Church is always itself but never the same)."

Early on, in the very beginning, there was a sense that what Jesus taught and did should be faithfully remembered but not repeated in the form the first disciples received it. The words and deeds of Jesus had to be applied concretely and creatively to conditions Jesus did not address.

And, so, apostolic imagination was born. What Jesus never directed became normative for the apostolic community.

- Gentiles were accepted as equal to Jews, by baptism
- A New Testament was written
- Four different Gospels interpreted Jesus in diverse ways
- A sacramental system developed
- There was a plurality of ministers based on charism and community approval
- Paul, who never met Jesus, is considered an apostle
- Women are given the title "apostle"
- The structure of "The Twelve," created by Jesus, and kept as "The Twelve" before Pentecost (Matthias succeeds Judas), is allowed to expire

Apostolic imagination worked in the apostolic age and continued through the first millenium.

- The liturgy is celebrated not in Aramaic but in Gentile languages in which Jesus did not pray
- Ecumenical Councils are inaugurated
- The Council of Nicea describes Jesus in ways he did not and would not use (the Son consubstantial with the Father)
- Ephesus describes Mary ("Mother of God") in language the first-century Church would reject
- Rome, not Jerusalem, becomes the mother Church

- The papacy is granted authority to function as Peter's successor

- Monasteries create communities of people who withdraw from everyday life in a manner Jesus did not endorse

The driving force behind apostolic imagination is two-fold.

In the first instance, the Spirit was believed to guide the Christian community in directions impossible to predict.

We have seen this operate in the first millennium. It continued in the second. There were two startling Ecumenical Councils in the second millenium. They were examples that apostolic imagination was still at work.

One of these was Constance, an assembly driven by the *sensus fidelium.* Although opposed by all three popes, it attributed its authority to the Holy Spirit. It took the institutional Church away from renegade popes and gave the People of God a pope they would accept.

Vatican II was a totally unprecedented Council. It was the first Council to abandon the juridical model and language of the Roman Empire's Senate. It issued no definitions, no denunciations, no infallible doctrines. It was the first Council to deal with the laity, as we have seen. It insisted the Church was the People of God. It declared the significance of the *sensus fidelium.*

Had the community been more prominent in the last fifty years, the Church would have been better guided.

- There would have been a different teaching on birth control

- and on a married priesthood

- and on the ordination of women

- and on same-sex relationships

- and on ecumenical unity
- and on the sexual abuse crisis
- and on fiscal accountability
- and on hierarchical mismanagement

Listen to what, now Blessed John Henry Newman, one of the greatest Catholic theologians in Church history, had to say in this regard. Long before a conciliar decree is issued, he observed, the laity accept it through the centuries by what might be called their "silent votes."

Later, commenting on the Arian heresy which tore the Church apart, not long after the New Testament was formulated, Newman notes: "the body of the episcopate was unfaithful to its commission while the body of the laity was faithful to its baptism . . . the pope. . . . said what (he) should not have said . . . the body of bishops failed. . . ." The Arian heresy was concerned with who Jesus of Nazareth was and how he should be defined. Newman makes clear that the official Church got the teaching on Christ wrong and that the *sensus fidelium* saved the Church. Because of this he tells us: "in order to know the tradition of the Apostles we must have recourse to the faithful."

We have now entered the third millennium. Of this we are certain. The Church will continue to go in directions no one can predict. It will, as it always has, declare as doctrine and law many things which are now condemned. The faithful at large will see to this. The third millennium gives us some indication that this will be the millennium of the Spirit and of the community. Much of the first millennium focused on who Christ is. Much of the second millennium dealt with how the institutional Church is defined. This millennium begins with the Spirit and the People of God.

The faith of the Church, we conclude, is not entrusted to a few but to all God's People. Once we lose sight of Luke's words that Pentecost was for "all," we create not a Pentecost Church but a Church without Pentecost where the doors are closed and fear locks the disciples into themselves.

In a Church without Pentecost, Jesus dies a second time, not on Calvary but in the midst of his own disciples.

A Church without Pentecost has place for a hierarchy but not for God's People. It gives us only memories of Jesus and takes away the community's ability to think in new ways.

Why would we want such a Church?

Clearly, Jesus did not.

Nor did the Spirit.

Why would we want such a Church?

Clearly, the apostles did not.

Nor did the New Testament.

**Why would we want such a Church?**

We would want such a Church only if we forget our beginnings, silence the culture of dialogue and forfeit apostolic imagination.

But then we have the Church of Christ no more. Without the People of God, the gates of hell prevail and the Church of Jesus Christ, the living Church of God's Spirit, is built no longer on rock but on sand.

In such a Church the apostles die in vain and the blood of martyrs is no longer the seed of the future.

**Why would we want such a Church?**

In such a Church, the waters of baptism make us only institutional Catholics and no longer the disciples of Christ.

**Why would we want such a Church?**

In such a Church the law matters more than the Gospel, and compliance takes precedence over faith, and we become a subservient community in which all but a few are slaves and serfs.

**Why would we want such a Church?**?

Clearly Christ did not want this. Nor do we.

We shall not become such a Church. In the name of God, for the sake of Christ, by the power of the Spirit, we ask for something better, braver, bolder, not for ourselves alone but for all God's People.

*Note: Two canon lawyers, Rick Torfs of Louvain, Belgium, and James Coriden of Washington, D.C. Theological Union, and one theologian, the Australian writer Ormond Rush, were guides in the writing of this essay.*

# Chapter Seven
# Encounters with Freedom

It happened swiftly, without warning, with a suddenness never before experienced in Church history. An ecumenical council was summoned, with no one calling for it, with no crisis on the horizon and without much of an agenda other than "updating." Yet there are those who claim it was the best of all councils.

Vatican II was the first ecumenical council to break away entirely from the juridical model used by the Senate of the Roman Empire. It jettisoned rigid legal categories and focused on being pastoral, practical, personal.

This Council changed our lives on almost every level imaginable. If you and I are to be named or identified, it must be done in terms of the Second Vatican Council.

Let us explore together two themes:

- The Magnitude of Vatican II

- Surviving Retrenchment

## The Magnitude of Vatican II

I would like to begin with a look at three time periods.

**The first of these is in the first century of our era.**
The event is the destruction of the Temple in Jerusalem. The immediate effects of this on Judaism are fourfold:

- The priesthood is eliminated
  Judaism shifts to teaching, pastoral care, family ritual, collective memory and finds it does quite well without a priesthood.

- There is no sacrifice

- There is no Temple or High Priest
  An entire centralizing substantial structure is gone.

- The Hebrew Bible becomes central
  The Bible is now the heritage, less of Scribes and scholars and more of the people.

**The second of these time periods is the Reformation.** The event is akin to a Christian destruction of the Temple. The immediate effects on Reformed Christianity are fourfold:

- The priesthood is eliminated
  Reformed Christianity shifts to teaching and pastoral care and finds it does quite well without a priesthood.

- There is no sacrifice
  The sacrifice of the Mass becomes a Communion Service around a table of full participation.

- There is no Vatican Temple or Pope as High Priest
  An entire centralizing substantial structure is gone.

- The New Testament becomes central
  Universal accessibility of the Gospel through the vernacular focuses on the Bible as the heritage of God's People.

**The third of these time periods is Vatican II.**
Catholicism moves, less radically but clearly, in the direction of Judaism and the Reformation.

- The priesthood is less necessary
  There is a shift to teaching and pastoral care by people at large and even their active presence in liturgical ritual.

- The Eucharist is less focused on sacrifice
  It is more often defined as a sacrament, a community celebration, done in memory of Christ.

- The Vatican and the Papacy become less obligatory
  These centralizing structures become less infallible, so to speak, less necessary for Catholics who define themselves as Catholics even as they reject Vatican direction and papal teaching.

- The New Testament becomes central
  Catholics find the New Testament more crucial than official Church teaching or an infallible magisterium; indeed all ecclesial policy lacks credibility unless it can be normed by the Gospel.

Vatican II ushered in the Third Millenium.

- **The First Millenium told us to listen to Christ.**
  The community was resilient and change was in the air. Gentiles, a written Gospel, a sacramental system, monasticism, ecumenical councils, the papacy were all put in place.

- **The Second Millenium asked us to listen to Church officers.**
  From Gregory VII early in the second millennium, claiming the pope answers only to God, to Vatican I and papal infallibility, Catholicism made Church teaching central. The result was not change but fracture: the Orthodox leave in the eleventh century; the Council of Constance moves against three popes simultaneously in office in the fifteenth century; the Reformers break away in the sixteenth; papal infallibility in the nineteenth century makes the structure more rigid and isolates it from the modern world.

- **The Third Millenium invites us to listen to the Spirit.**
  The least juridical of councils is convened as a new Pentecost for the Church; the Spirit is everywhere as Catholics hear the once unknown languages of the world, the other religions, the alternative Christian

Churches and the way people speak and believe when they are not formal administrators of the Church.

- **What did the Council do?**
  I was at St. Paul's in Rome when John XXIII announced Vatican II on January 25, 1959, in that very church. I did not know it then but a year before ordination to the priesthood my life had been changed irreversibly.

  A Council had been called. The city of Rome was filled with shock, surprise, and suspense. The Council had no agenda. It was all very amorphous. This vagueness made creativity possible. So the Council moved into poetry rather than prose, spirituality rather than doctrine. It would not be militantly against adversaries. It would be on the side of God's People. It would listen to the Spirit.

  The Council created 16 documents (seven of them were pivotal). These seven, I maintain, would resist the forces of retrenchment and would also prove relevant around the world and across the generations.

Seven documents went right to the heart of the Church and opened up the future in a remarkable manner.

What are these seven documents?

- Four were Constitutions (Liturgy, Church, Revelation, the Modern World)

- One was a Decree (Ecumenism)

- Two were Declarations (World Religions; Religious Freedom)

I shall synthesize the charge that came from these seven documents in five themes.

## CHANGE THE LITURGY (LITURGY CONSTITUTION)

The Council moved the Liturgy from Rome (Latin) to our own culture (vernacular). It moved it from the priest (Latin, back to people, communion rail, no touching of chalice or bread, silent congregations, obligatory attendance) to the people (who plan and participate, respond and sing, take communion into their hands, read and minister communion to others). All this has held. Non-ordained, baptized Christians lead Sunday communion services. And some reform Catholics do not hesitate to celebrate Eucharist with no ordained priest presiding.

We may disagree with the Vatican about rubrics or translations now but we feel free to dissent because we sense the Liturgy is ours and not only theirs. These disagreements are not unimportant but they are minor compared to what has been accomplished. The conflict shows the Council took. Liturgy has been irreversibly reinterpreted.

## CHANGE THE CHURCH (*LUMEN GENTIUM*)

The Church is no longer papacy and hierarchy but the People of God. We expect Church officials to speak in the language of Scripture, not that of the Magisterium, and in the inclusive language of democracy, "We the People." If this lacking many we choose not to listen.

Vatican II issued no dogmas, no definitions. In this first council after the declaration of papal infallibility, it declared nothing infallible and it did not reference papal infallibility to support its decisions. Indeed the pope was not present during the deliberations or the final voting. The pope approved nothing the assembly did not endorse. He gave a final signature the way a democratic American president does. He did not venture into the legislative assembly, so to speak, just as an American president does not enter into the debates going on in Congress. Watching Vatican II, one would not conclude the papacy was infallible. Indeed, as late as 1959, the consensus among Catholic theologians and bishops was that there would never be another Council since the pope was declared infallible a century before at Vatican I. The assumption was that the vast machinery of the ecumenical council was no longer necessary. The pope alone could teach us efficiently and infallibly. The very existence of Vatican II undermined and restricted the doctrine of papal infallibility.

Every key issue passed by Vatican II, all of them by lopsided majorities, would have been resoundingly defeated as late as 1962. A number of the final documents would have been condemned as schismatic or heretical. They are now official Church policy.

At the end of Vatican II in 1965, the Catholic Church had been changed forever. It would not and could not reverse course in any substantial way. That was over. The revolution and the reform were on the record, overwhelmingly endorsed, and, indeed, embedded in the minds and hearts of people, including conservatives. It was so deeply present in the community that even reactionaries who attacked the Council and young people who were unaware of it or saw it as irrelevant do not realize how they have been changed by it. It was over. Latin Masses are not popular; they seem a curiosity. A reactionary pope would apologize to Muslims and Jews, enter their mosques and synagogues, pray with Protestants. Imagine a Pope praying with Protestants, publicly, and even honoring Martin Luther's birthday before Vatican II. It was over.

Imagine a meeting, as late as 1965, with married priests (an oxymoron) and their wives, together with priests in canonical standing, Protestant Christians, same-sex couples, organizing strategies against Vatican policy, planning and celebrating Mass as they deem appropriate. The questions now about whether we would attend such a conference would concern whether we had the time or the money or what the program was and who the speakers were. We do not wonder whether Catholics should be at such a meeting.

In January of 2010, when I was in Rome for the fiftieth ordination anniversary of my class, we were all invited by the Pope to a private audience in which he greeted each one of us personally. He did not send word before that married priests were not welcome or their wives excluded. Nor did he limit married priests in attendance only to those canonically dispensed or only to those who were not organized in groups resisting Vatican policy. It never occurred to anyone to exclude anyone. And this Pope is a conservative.

## CHANGE THE MAGISTERIUM (REVELATION CONSTITUTION)

We have gone from a rigorous exegesis of papal encyclicals in 1959 to a virtual neglect of them. Papal teaching was once more decisive than the New Testament or Tradition. Indeed, we now feel comfortable rejecting papal encyclicals outright (*Humanae Vitae*) and papal teaching completely. The recent ordinations of women and the best theology written on ordaining women happened after the solemn decision of John Paul II, appealing to his apostolic authority, to prohibit the ordination of women. The vast majority of Catholics who agree women should be ordained has increased since that decree.

We have gone, conservatives and liberals, from hearing the Pope so we could get a sense of what direction we should follow to deciding whether we agree with the Pope or not.

The norms that mean the most for Catholics now, conservatives and liberals, are the Gospel (what Jesus did) and conscience (what I must do). Both meant less than the Magisterium in 1962. Before Vatican II, Catholics accepted conscience only if it was normed by the Magisterium and only if it was used as a last resort against a church official who ordered them to do something clearly sinful. Conscience was then exotic, extreme, unreliable and even somehow suspiciously Protestant.

## CHANGE THE RELATIONSHIP WITH THE WORLD (*GAUDIUM ET SPES*)

The world does not serve the Church (Middle Ages) nor is the Church above the world (papal monarchy). The Church is in the modern world. Indeed, we have learned since Vatican II that the major ethical and social issues of our time have been set by the world:

- The role of women
- Reproductive issues

- Same-sex relationships
- Democracy in Church and State
- The right to divorce whether we call it annulment or not
- The elimination of mandatory celibacy
- Charters of human rights (U.S. Constitution; United Nations; European Union)
- Abandonment of capital punishment

Catholics, by and large, find more wisdom in the world than in the papacy or in the institutional Church. Compare, for example, the great charters on human rights I cited a moment earlier with the restricted rights listed in the 1983 Code of Canon Law. It is naïve to suppose that the world alone is a safe haven for humanity. But the Church alone is also an unsafe place.

The Spirit, I suggest, is not less present anywhere in the world than it is in the Church. The human heart carries the Holy Spirit. Wherever the human heart is safe, in the world or in the Church, there God is with us.

The world, therefore, is not evil or a vale of tears, but a sanctuary where life develops and the future is open-ended and hope is endless. Catholics at large, conservatives and liberals, would be terrified to be left to the mercy of the Church, without the world as an alternative. Just about every married priest and pastor, the victims of sexual abuse, and many Catholics in troubled marriages found justice in the world and little of it in the Church.

The Church, nonetheless, is not to be the world's slave but its partner. The world at large does not listen to the pope but it is moved by the Church at large and the social justice of committed Catholics. Whenever the Church is authentic, the world hears it. Whenever the Church is a fraud, the world persecutes it. The Holocaust would have been stopped if millions of Catholic laity, priests and bishops and the pope with them, surrounded the ghettoes and stood on the railroad tracks and demanded that the concentration camps be closed.

The call to holiness is not only in the Church but in the worldly lives we live with decency and grace. The parables of Jesus are not about the Church or Temple but about our worldly lives.

## CHANGE OUR DEFINITION OF THE SACRED (ECUMENISM, WORLD RELIGIONS, RELIGIOUS FREEDOM)

The Decree on Ecumenism declared Orthodox and Protestant communities sacred institutions, not schismatic or heretical but capable of bringing Christ to their believing members.

The Declaration on World Religions found Hinduism, Buddhism, Judaism, and Islam sources of truth and love. The Pope invited representatives of the world religions to come to Assisi and pray with him and he visited their sacred places. Catholic monks and priests, nuns and people at large made retreats and became community members of other than Christian assemblies.

The Declaration on Religious Freedom declared conscience sacred.

The sacred shifted from a pre-Copernican universe with an infallible and immovable Catholic Church at its center to a post-Copernican cosmos with God alone at its center and an ecclesial planetary system of sacred bodies, all in motion, none without light, none able to replace the other or become a center for it. Conscience brings us to the religion God has given us as the religion we must choose for ourselves. A religion is sacred, not because it is right or true, but because it has the capacity to reach our hearts at a deeper spiritual level than any other religion.

The magnitude of Vatican II has been underestimated, even by the reformers. Has the Council held? Of course, it has. Our memories fail to recall how different we once were.

- In January, (2010), in Rome, I was present for the 150th anniversary of North American College, and the most reactionary bishops and cardinals celebrated some of the major liturgies for us; yet all celebrated in English even though all of us knew Latin, faced the congregation, gave communion in the hand inclusively to all who came forward; the homilies and ceremonies were little different from what we would say or do at a Catholic reform meeting.

- It is virtually impossible, around the world, to find reactionary scholars or Church officers who will publicly debate mandatory celibacy, sexual ethics, the ordination of women and so on; they know the official teaching on these issues is simply not credible and they are reluctant to be publicly embarrassed by defending the indefensible; instead, they retreat to edicts or monologues.

- Reactionaries have lost their courage and are frightened; the future does not belong to the fearful.

- A Catholic who married a Protestant in 1962, with Church approval, was barred from the Catholic Church and married in the Rectory, without the blessing of the rings, without communion or even the possibility of having a nuptial Mass; today, a Catholic may marry, with full endorsement, in a Catholic or Protestant Church, presided over by a minister and a priest; with communion for both partners and a nuptial Mass; with the baptism of the Protestant partner fully recognized and the Protestant tradition honored; all of this happens with hardly a second thought.

- Catholics who practiced birth control in 1962, in large numbers, were almost universally convinced they were doing something seriously wrong even if their conscience told them they often had no other choice; now Catholics, almost universally, are convinced that birth control is their decision, and that the pope is seriously wrong.

- Catholics in 1962 felt an obligation to think and act the way the pope directed, if they would be good Catholics and continue to receive communion; now, as good Catholics, receiving communion, they feel no disconnect in demanding that the pope resign, cardinals be dismissed, and bishops or priests put in prison.

- The priest shortage has come about because Catholics, conservatives as strongly as liberals, refuse the priesthood, in overwhelming numbers, if it is offered on the terms the Magisterium presents; the shortage will end, immediately, if Gospel norms and conscience are respected in the selection process.

There is no future in reactionary Catholicism. The Council has held; young people find it in the *zeitgeist* and in the world they inhabit; the essence of the Council is embedded in the truth and wisdom and life of the human family and the signs of our times. It is all inescapable now. Where the world fails, authentic Catholics will speak out; where the Church fails, the world will correct it. This is what the Incarnation and the gift of the Spirit mean for our age.

Indeed, Catholics disregard Church officials when they no longer have common sense and when what they say violates the sacred core of a believer. The Spirit does not require official Church approval before it creates new life, a new Christianity, and a new world.

## Surviving Retrenchment

An issue of critical importance for many reformers is how we survive the retrenchment. The major levers of power and decision-making have been seized by reactionaries.

In order to evaluate this sad turn of events, it is necessary to give it context. The reforms have won the minds and hearts of people. Even conservatives will not support a pre-Vatican II Church without taking many of the reforms with them. They have lost the memory of a Church without any of these reforms. There is no going back even among those who want to go back.

There are signs of a radically changed mentality everywhere.

- Conservatives as well as liberals want church officials punished for sex abuse and its cover-up; they are not as sure as they once were that their children are safe in the institutional Church.

- As we have seen, very few Catholics want to become priests; most Catholics envision or expect priests to resign; divorce and birth control are as common among conservative as among liberal Catholics.

- There is widespread indifference to official Church teaching and frequent hostility to it.

- Docility and Church attendance are as rare among young conservatives as among young liberal Catholics; indeed, both camps show a tolerance of what their parents may have seen as aberrant behavior.

- The number of times a pope, Benedict XVI, has apologized on a whole array of issues is unprecedented in Church history; even he is embarrassed and defensive about his own behavior in regulating abusive priests.

The retrenchment is not working except on the level of power and intimidation. The truth, however, cannot be controlled by a police-state mentality. The Spirit is not limited to the categories and boundaries foolish people draw.

Today, there is a sense that no healthy person would choose to preside over, live, and work, in such an unstable and unreal environment. The defense and promotion of this system now requires a pathological mentality and a corruption of the truth.

How do we survive the interim until this season of darkness and discontent passes? I suggest four strategies.

## Conscience

Conscience is not an absolute norm so that it can stand on its own. But it is an absolutely indispensable norm.

Conscience inspired resistance and integrity when Nazi and Communist officials seized the levers of power and decision-making. It can do the same when Church officials put in place a police-state. They do this because they despair that the truth is able to support their policies. In this, they are right.

Conscience has deep Catholic roots. It is essential to authenticity, grounded in a call to holiness and fundamental to personal identity. Nothing can even begin to take its place. Henry David Thoreau once asked: if doing what others want me to do is sufficient, then why did each of us get a conscience?

Thomas Aquinas said that a person is obliged to do an evil deed, if that person believes in conscience, it is a good deed. No one, he continued, has the right to obey an unjust law or to follow false teaching. Even if we give our minds and wills to official teaching we must not let our consciences go there as readily.

Luther was a Catholic and a monk, taught by Augustine and Aquinas, when he proclaimed that he had to follow his conscience and could not do otherwise. Everyone who knew the Catholic Tradition understood that.

John Henry Newman wrote:

> "[in a] collision with the word of a pope . . . [conscience] is to be followed in spite of that word."

He called conscience the "Vicar of Christ" for each of us. And he famously toasted conscience first and the pope second.

Vatican II gave Catholics their consciences back, so to speak, after Pius IX, Pius X and later John Paul II worked to diminish conscience in favor of absolute claims for the Magisterium.

In "The Church in the Modern World" we read:

> "Deep within conscience, people discover a law they have not laid on themselves but which must be obeyed. Its voice, ever calling to love and to what is good ... tells us inwardly at the right moment: do this, shun that. Human dignity lies in observing this law ... There we are alone with God whose voice echoes in us ... conscience joins Christians to others in our common search for truth."

Understanding the Council, then, Joseph Ratzinger wrote in 1967:

> "Over the pope ... there stands ... conscience which must be obeyed before all else, even if necessary against the requirement of ecclesiastical authority."

Conscience, of course, should seek development and enter into dialogue with the human family and with the decency and wisdom there. Conscience is always a work in progress but it is always mine. If I lose conscience, I lose everything of value, my identity, and my integrity and people at large know this when they meet me. I forfeit my spiritual calling for a bowl of porridge and a handful of dust.

## FRIENDSHIP

Cicero (106-43 B.C.E.; 63 years) wrote two literally unforgettable essays: one on aging and one on friendship. They are compatible and I would like to consider them together.

Cicero, who died half a century before Jesus was born, is a concrete example of the wisdom in the human family that does not need Christianity to make it happen.

A word about Cicero. Two years before his death, his daughter Tullia died, in 45 B.C. E. He is devastated by the loss and it ages him. Her death occurs in a season of discontent. He is disappointed that the promise of Julius Caesar's leadership has drifted into dictatorship. Cicero feels isolated as so many of his colleagues go with those in power, against a truth they once affirmed.

I might cover these essays best by giving you a running narrative of how they go, with quotes every so often.

> I'm feeling old, he tells us. Not as active as I once was. I comfort myself with the thought that a tiller of a ship does not do less in bringing a ship to harbor, even if he is not as active as the younger sailors. I think about death more frequently now and I know it is near. Yet even the young have no guarantees. One learns to be grateful and to build a legacy of memories and good deeds.
>
> Friendship is my deepest comfort. My friends are no longer the colleagues who once advanced my career but companions whose presence brings me peace. I do not choose them for their cleverness or their knowledge but simply for their presence.
>
> Friends make me patient with my life, tolerant of its losses and ambiguities, accepting of the compromises we sometimes need to make so that others can live. They teach me to accept the folly of life without blaming others or holding myself to some impossible standard. We who have aged have been tested and endured, failed and persevered, were rejected and survived. We learn to live with gratitude. The good we did will endure forever.

The only gift, Cicero observes, that will enable me to have no regrets at the end is friendship. He defines friendship as a "complete sympathy in all matters of importance." And he adds that life is not worth living without it.

Cicero fell out of favor with Roman authorities and was executed, at the age of 63, in 43 B.C.E., one year after the assassination of Julius Caesar. No one reads the writings of those then in power, to gain comfort from them. The words of Cicero remain.

Thomas Aquinas (1225-1274: 49 years), a singularly unemotional writer, wrote this:

> " . . . without friends, even the most agreeable pursuits become tedious."

And this:

> "There is nothing on this earth more to be prized than true friendship."

In summary, conscience gives me myself; friendship brings me the other.

## Vision

What do we want the institutional Church to be or do for us?

It cannot settle my conscience or select my friends.

I do not want the institutional Church to be a teacher but a partner; not a total system, but an occasional source of insight.

It cannot give me Christ or the Spirit; I have them already.

It can help me achieve some of the values I learn about in the Church: social justice or spirituality. But I always find Catholics and others who have the same vision even if the institution would not recommend them to me.

And so, I, we, give a fair amount of energy to creative resistance. We do this because we believe the institutional Church is worth it and because something–God or conscience or the truth or friendship—something calls us to do this. Surprisingly, creative resistance has given us depth. We would have been superficial Catholics and less profoundly human without it.

John O'Mally S.J. gives us a litany about what Vatican II tried to do and what reform seeks to do. It resonates with young people as well as with their elders. It moves all of us from:

- monologue to dialogue
- command to invitation

- law to ideals
- coercion to conscience
- ruling to serving
- threats to persuasion
- behavior modification to inner conviction
- hostility to friendship
- the static to the ongoing
- rivalry to partnership
- suspicion to trust

I believe that I am truly Catholic when I do not need the institutional Church to validate me. I find this in my conscience, my friends, my vision.

I do not need the institutional Church to agree with me but to let go of trying to control me. I am happy to have it speak to me but then leave me to my autonomy. I need the institutional Church not to need to make me needy.

I need the institutional Church to stop trying to become a nursing home where eventually all my requirements are addressed by others and I become helpless. (I am not against nursing homes; but they are not a future one chooses but a present one settles for). To put able-bodied and mentally sound people in a nursing home is an outrage.

The institutional Church has a value and plays a role in our lives and in the life of the world. It is worth reforming because it is so massive in its potential influence and so rich in the gifts of its Tradition and sacraments. But it can never play a significant role in my life unless it takes my life seriously. The same rule applies to a spouse, a parent or a friend.

Judiciously selective Catholicism is the only way to become a comprehensive Catholic; such Catholicism respects conscience and the integrity of others. Total Catholicism is toxic. It makes the Church a slave plantation and it is terrified by the thought of freedom. Reforming the institutional Church is another form of abolition. Jesus of Nazareth called us to discipleship, not serfdom.

I remain certain of a few truths abut the Church:

- It will continue to change.
- The model for that change will be Vatican II.
- The change will move broadly in the direction the Catholic reform movement has indicated.

I am certain of these truths because the vast majority of Catholics are there and because the young are there in overwhelming numbers even if they do not use ecclesial, theological, or conciliar language.

Does anyone, with any sense, really think that women or homosexuals will have fewer rights in the future, or that the prohibition on birth control will be endorsed or that the Christian Churches will grow farther apart or that the papacy will ever again have the control it did between the Council of Trent and Vatican II or that mature people in the world will turn over to the Vatican the full responsibility for deciding who they are, what they believe, how they behave and all that it means to be a Catholic?

Does anyone really think the future will go there?

## Witness

So suppose you are a Roman Catholic bishop now.

- Would you be happy?
- No one listens.

- The world is elsewhere.

- Catholics are not even in line on abortion.

- You have to speak regularly against common sense, your conscience and what you know is the better pastoral approach.

- Hardly anyone wants to become a priest and many who do are people you would not have wanted as your pastor when you began ministry.

- You feel you cannot trust or rely on laity or priests; and you are suspicious of many of your bishop colleagues.

- You are expected to police who is coming to communion.

- You have to watch the rubrics in the Liturgy like a hawk so that it is seldom an act of worship and a peaceful experience.

- There are adversaries everywhere as you see it: media, the modern world, relativists, Catholic theologians, books in general, nuns in particular.

- You have to play a role that is so scripted that they give you no lines for your own part.

- The chancery has become a bunker.

- The sex abuse cases may have at least two more generations to go.

- Everyone looks forward to your retirement or resignation.

- Liberals are everywhere.

- You know you are not winning; you are shot through with anxiety rather than tranquil confidence.

So now let us be ourselves.

- Vatican II is a charter for Selective Catholicism. **This is our witness.**

- We do what we do because we find it full of meaning. **This is our witness.**

- We give our lives to exactly the kind of vision we affirm. **This is our witness.**

- We find freedom and peace in this spiritual journey. **This is our witness.**

- We live without dishonesty and cravenness, without fear or against conscience. **This is our witness.**

- What we stand for in public is what we stand for in private. **This is our witness.**

- We proclaim that Vatican II was not for the hierarchy (they have lost control since then) and not for the papacy (the pope is less influential since then). **This is our witness.**

- We demonstrate that Vatican II was about people at large, the laity or baptized Christians; it was about community. **This is our witness.**

- We shall be Catholics for as long as we live, on our own terms, not without partners and dialogue but without intimidation and servility. **This is our witness.**

- We are the daughters and sons, the heirs and heralds of Vatican II. **This is our witness.**

- We shall be faithful to all we have learned and experienced from our relationship with Christ and with friends, from the wisdom we gathered by the lives we have lived.
**This is our witness.**

- We shall go on, unvanquished and invincible, for the sake of our friends and our family, for the sake or our children and grandchildren, for the sake of the Gospel and the Spirit who brought us here to this point.
**This is our witness.**

- We shall not falter and we shall not fail because we seek a future that includes everyone, one from which no one is rejected, the kind of a future that once made Christ send us to the ends of the earth and led the early Church to embrace the Gentiles.
**This is our witness.**

- Almost no one instinctively defines the institutional Catholic Church as a compassionate community; we seek to change that.
**This is our witness.**

- All of this is not about ourselves but about a Christ whose life makes us breathless with wonder and a God who has never let go of us, a God we believe reaches out to everyone, a Spirit who makes us restless and sets us on fire, a fire that cannot be quenched because it is the fire of love itself, the fire that moves the sun and the cosmos and all the stars.
**This is our witness.**

- We shall exclude no one except those who choose not to join us.
**This is our witness.**

- We go forward neither frightened, intimidated nor doubtful but stalwart and steadfast, not because we suppose we are superior but because we are convinced we

have been summoned.
**This is our witness.**

So be it. In the name of Christ.